PONY MADNESS

Rita Lyttle

Pony Madness

Illustrated by Paul Geraghty

Hodder & Stoughton

LONDON SYDNEY AUCKLAND TORONTO

British Library Cataloguing in Publication Data

Lyttle, Rita
  Pony madness.
  I. Title   II. Geraghty, Paul
  823'.914[J]   PZ7
    ISBN 0-340-41127-9

Published by Hodder and Stoughton Children's Books,
a division of Hodder and Stoughton Ltd,
Mill Road, Dunton Green, Sevenoaks, Kent TN13 2YJ

Photoset by Rowland Phototypesetting Ltd,
Bury St Edmunds, Suffolk

Printed in Great Britain by T. J. Press (Padstow) Ltd,
Padstow, Cornwall

One

It was only five minutes to the end of the road if she ran as fast as she could, and from there it was possible to see right down the hillside to the stable-yard beyond, and the field where Merlin waited. Lissa had just decided that she could slip away for one last look when her mother's frantic voice echoed up the stairway:

'Lissa! What are you doing? It's time to go.'

So here it was, the final moment. So many things had happened in this room, so many thoughts, so many plans, but now there was nothing left to remind her, for the walls were stripped bare with only the pale shadows remaining.

Goodbye room. Goodbye old stairs. Goodbye front door. The house was a stranger, with all their belongings, all the furniture and curtains gone so that even their own voices sounded as though they belonged to someone else.

'Hurry up!' Mrs Tallis cried. 'We must get there before the removal van and I don't want to drive too fast.' She was waiting in the rain and her hair was wet.

Lissa climbed into the back seat where Cass was curled up in the opposite corner, with a blanket pulled up over her nose, and Ginny was squashed in the middle, looking pale and anxious. Mrs Tallis banged the front door and walked quickly round to the neighbour to leave the house keys. At the sound of the door banging, Lissa shut her eyes tightly and slumped back in her seat, feeling numb. Any last hope that something might happen to change things, that they might not have to leave after all, was finally gone. The weeks of dread seemed to come to a head in this single moment.

She glanced over at Cass who looked back at her quite calmly, then reached into a pocket and brought out a small brown envelope. Inside was a bundle of thick black hair, tied up with a blue ribbon. Lissa stared.

'It's Merlin's,' Cass said.

'Oh, Cass!' Lissa cried, gratefully. Sometimes Cass did the most wonderful things. She always seemed to have the knack of doing just the right thing at the right moment. Lissa sniffed the bundle, but it smelt only of lemon.

'Sorry, but I washed it in washing-up liquid,' Cass said sleepily, then shut her eyes and prepared to sleep.

'Oh. Thank you, anyway.'

Cassandra was only ten, a year younger than Lissa, yet they were nearly the same height; Cass was tall and skinny, and Lissa was slightly small for her age. But they had the same fair hair and brown skin. Lissa wondered how Cass could simply shut her eyes and go to sleep at a time like this, even though they had been up since five o'clock.

At last they were on the road. 'Oh, what a relief!' Mrs Tallis said. 'The first part is over. I thought we'd never get away.'

'How long will it take?' asked Ginny.

'About four hours in this old car. I only hope it doesn't break down. We'll stop once or twice, but I don't want to take too long, we can't keep the men waiting. I just wish today was over.'

'I wish we could have said goodbye to the ponies,' said Lissa.

'You said goodbye yesterday,' her mother replied.

'It's not the same, It's today we're moving.'

'They won't know.'

'We will,' Cassandra murmured.

'If only it wasn't so far away,' Lissa muttered. Then she and Cass could have come back, at least at weekends, to the stables where they had both been helping for the last two years.

It still seemed unbelievable that they would get up on a Saturday morning and have no stables to go to, no Mrs Harrison shouting at them to hurry up with the haynets, no tack-cleaning sessions in the evening with Pat and, worst of all, no Merlin.

Lissa loved all the ponies, especially Poppy, the Welsh Mountain pony on whom they had both learnt to ride, even if she did take a nip at everyone occasionally, or take charge sometimes if she got bored on a rather slow hack. There was Clara, the elegant part Arab that Lissa admired with awe, for she had only recently been allowed to ride her for the first time. And then there was Merlin.

Merlin was something different. He and Lissa had formed an attachment that she had never known with any other animal. He had a coat as sleek and shiny as a dark brown mole, with the markings of an Exmoor pony, neat black legs, a thick curly mane perched on a strong neck, a beautiful face touched by a small white star, and a soft velvety muzzle that searched her face and hands for affection. He was 14.2 hands, rather large for Lissa really; he loved to work and he loved to jump even though he was still young.

She imagined Merlin waiting at the fence for her as he

always did, bewildered when she never turned up. He would wait there for hours as he did whenever she left him to go home, his face lifted long after she reached the end of the drive and climbed the hill, when she would steal a last glimpse of him before turning into the lane. Thinking about Merlin, Lissa felt a heavy pain in her chest. She felt hot tears on her cheeks and put her head forward so that her hair fell over her face to hide them.

'Are you all right, Lissa?' her mother asked and looking up, Lissa met her eyes in the driving-mirror. She could not speak for a minute, but nodded.

'Are you hungry? You'll find some biscuits in the blue carrier.'

'I feel sick,' announced Ginny from the middle where she sat hunched up in misery and squashed between her two sisters. She was the youngest, only six years old. She had dark, shoulder-length hair like her mother's only it was parted on one side and clipped on the other with a hairslide shaped like a butterfly. Her small curly mouth turned down sharply at the corners, rather like a cartoon character, Lissa always thought. She did look awfully white, though. Lissa hoped she was not going to be sick all over her.

'Not long now,' Mrs Tallis was saying cheerfully. 'Have a peppermint.'

Presently the sky cleared a little, and the rain eased, so they pulled off the road for a picnic.

'I wish I had my drawing-book,' said Cassandra, climbing up the bank for a better view of the surrounding scenery. She always liked to look around as she enjoyed painting and making sketches of the places they passed through. Now, however, her materials were lost in the chaos inside the furniture van.

'What's my bedroom going to be like, Mummy?' Ginny asked. After running up and down for a while she was feeling better, and sat on a stile to eat her sandwich.

'I haven't seen any of the bedrooms, so I can't tell you. But the downstairs is lovely. There's a big sitting-room with an open fireplace, they had a big log fire going when I went there with your father a few years ago; and the outside is nice too. There are lots of trees, and they used to have ducks and geese running around. I know you're going to like it.'

If their father hadn't been killed in the helicopter accident five years earlier they would never have had to move house at all. They could have stayed in their own home forever. But the money was gradually used up and the expenses of running the house became too high, and in the end the situation got quite desperate. Every time a brown envelope came through the letter-box, Mrs Tallis was cast into gloom for days on end; sometimes the telephone was cut off because the bill was unpaid. School clothes were a constant problem and shopping expeditions a nightmare. Then one day Mrs Tallis announced that it couldn't go on. They would have to leave their house and find somewhere much cheaper, but that had proved to be very difficult indeed.

And so it was that Mrs Tallis wrote to their grandfather for help, and after five years of bad fortune, they had their first piece of good luck, the timing was perfect. Apparently the old tenant who lived at the smallholding had just retired and gone to live with his sister. Their grandfather wrote and told them that there was no one else to leave the place to, so they might as well have it now when they needed it, although he did warn them that it had been rather neglected recently as old Tom had not been fit enough to look after it properly. Finally, however, all the arrangements were made for them to move in, and when the time came the keys were sent. So, here they were in no-man's-land, speeding off into the unknown, feeling as though they didn't belong anywhere.

It was only mid-afternoon, but it was getting very dark and presently the rain came pouring down again. They hastily picked everything up, piled back in the car and prepared to set off again.

'Are we nearly there?' Ginny asked.

'Over half way,' Mrs Tallis said, as she drove back on to the road. Another hour passed, during which the children mostly slept, and then they were through the last of the built-up areas around London and truly in the country again.

When Lissa next opened her eyes, the first thing she saw was a large sign saying: BEWARE OF SHEEP, DEER, HORSES. Glades of giant chestnuts and beech trees towered on both sides, now dotted with the yellow buds of spring. Between the glades vast rolling hills and forests stretched away into the distance, glimpsed now and then as the screens of heavy grey cloud lifted for a moment. The rain was now a slight drizzle. Mrs Tallis pulled into a lay-by to check the address and the map.

'Where are we?' asked Cass, opening her eyes and yawning.

'We're almost there. Your grandfather said to take the first left after the hill, which I hope means the one in front of us. Then it's only about another mile.'

They found the place quite easily. The name White Trees Farm was painted on a board propped against a large boulder in front of a crumbling gatepost, whilst the gate itself lay in ruins on the bank. Grass and brambles tore at the car as they drove through.

Lissa glanced at her mother in the driving-mirror. She had an anxious frown on her face, which she rapidly changed to a smile when she realised Lissa was watching. The smile vanished, though, when they finally came to a stop next to the furniture van in a small yard overgrown by shoulder-high weeds. They were facing a dark, rather forbidding-looking house, with water pouring from a broken gutter, and peeling paintwork. An upstairs window was broken. A chill came over them all and for a long time nobody wanted to move.

'It didn't look like this!' Mrs Tallis said, several times. At last she pulled herself together, saying 'Well, we were warned that it's been neglected. We'll just have to work hard and get it into shape.'

Cass was the first to move. She got out of the car and went to stand in the porch for shelter. From here she could survey the whole sorry scene of the dripping wilderness in front and the stark shell of a building all around.

'Do we have to stay here?' Ginny wailed, looking up at the black, curtainless windows.

'For now we do, my darling, but don't worry, we'll soon get it really cosy, you'll see. Just think how lucky we are to have a home of our own.'

'Well, I'd rather be back home.' Ginny said obstinately.

'So would we all, darling, but home no longer belongs to us and now we've got to make the best of it. You too.'

Lissa said nothing. As the eldest she knew she had to support her mother, who must be feeling as miserable as the rest of them, so she opened the boot of the car and started unloading. She felt cold and stiff and wretched.

Mrs Tallis ransacked her bag for the doorkey and, after opening the front door, went to speak to the removal

men who still sat in the front of their van, munching sandwiches and seeming in no hurry to get started.

'It's a pretty porch,' Cass remarked, looking up at the carvings which supported the small tiled roof, as she helped Lissa to carry everything from the car into the house.

'Yuk!' Lissa replied. 'Come on, let's explore.'

Together they ran from room to room. 'It smells!' Lissa remarked with distaste. Everywhere paper was peeling from the walls, leaving large black patches of mildew.

'It's been shut up for ages. Let's open some windows,' Cass suggested. Soon a fresh breeze was blowing through. Up the large wooden staircase they found a large bedroom at the front, two smaller ones at the back of the house, a bathroom with an ancient, white bath with lots of pipes everywhere, and then a tiny staircase winding up again to a large attic which ran nearly the length of the house.

'Oh! Look at the view,' Cass cried. Between the over-hanging trees and banks of grey cloud, a distant landscape in varying shades of grey could be seen.

'I want this room,' Cass said. Lissa just shrugged because there was nothing she wanted at that moment except to wake up out of a bad dream and find herself at home in bed, about to spend a day at the stables. In a moment, Mrs Tallis entered the room. Her forced cheerfulness was beginning to wear thin and she sounded tired. It was damp everywhere and very cold.

'We certainly can't sleep upstairs tonight,' she said. 'We can all camp in the living-room until the bedrooms can be aired. We'll find some way of making it warm.'

The three men were instructed to put all the upstairs furniture in the large bedroom and all the rest at one end of the living-room to give them time to sort it all out. Next, Mrs Tallis found the box with the tea-making things in it and went to put the kettle on. They all sat around glumly sipping strong tea from large mugs while the men made sympathetic noises.

'You'll need some help sorting this lot out,' one of them said. He was called Harry and had curly, red hair which was now very wet from his various journeys to and from the van.

'It will be all right in time,' said Mrs Tallis briskly. There was not any help, all they had was themselves. For a moment Lissa felt a flash of anger towards her grandfather, although she knew it was unfair. He had not seen the farm for years, so he could not possibly know what it was like; besides, her mother was surely right, after an awful lot of work and effort, this place could be made like a home.

Since it was rather chilly, and Lissa had noticed that

most of the rooms had fireplaces, she decided to put on a coat and look for firewood in one of the outhouses. The back door from the kitchen led into a brick courtyard and on one side was a kind of long, open shed with some machinery in it; here Lissa found a pile of old logs, already sawn. She filled her arms with as many as she could carry and took them back inside. There was a lot of newspaper used for wrapping things up for the journey, and she rolled several pieces together just as her father had shown her. One of the men helped her to bank up the fire, then he took out his lighter and lit one corner. In no time at all there was a fine blaze going and immediately the room looked more friendly. Everyone was delighted.

It was getting quite late when everything was at last unloaded, and finally the men left, with much shaking of heads and murmurs of sympathy. When they had gone, the house suddenly became very quiet and the Tallis family sat around the fire, not really wanting to unpack any further. Eventually Mrs Tallis stirred:

'Right you lot, it's half past six. This room is where we're going to sleep tonight, so let's make it as nice as we can.'

They arranged the two armchairs together for Ginny to sleep in; the settee was made up for Lissa; Cass and her mother piled up some bedding in a space on the floor and made a comfortable nest there. Lissa found the coffee-table, and Cass surprised everybody by filling a glass jar with daffodils from the garden, which cheered the room up a great deal. They found the overnight bag packed with soap and toothbrushes, and by quarter past seven they were ravenously hungry. Mrs Tallis said the two older girls could have fifteen minutes outside to explore while she made supper, and found the plates and cutlery. Everything else could wait until morning. Ginny was already asleep in the armchairs.

'You'll find your wellingtons in the wicker basket with the rest of the shoes,' their mother said. 'And do put your macs on. It's very wet everywhere.'

Outside, the air tasted very fresh and sweet. The clouds had drawn back to the top of the sky into streaks which caught the pink and gold of the setting sun. Over in the east it was still raining somewhere, and that was where they saw the rainbow, a clear, perfect arc of every colour with a vivid band of red on top, the piercing colours reaching almost into the garden. It grew even as they watched into a double rainbow, then, faintly, a third appeared. They felt drops of rain on their faces even though the sky above was now almost clear.

'It's a good sign,' Cass cried joyfully. 'Everything is going to be all right.'

Together they watched the rainbow until it began to fade, and then went on with the exploring.

From the front of the house, where the car was parked, an overgrown path forked in two directions; one following the line of the hedge round the side of the house behind the kitchen and ending in a small door which was locked, the other leading through a small gate in the hedge itself. As they forced open the rusty catch, a thousand drops of rain fell on them from the overhanging twigs and they were glad to be wearing macs. On the other side of the hedge they walked between gnarled old trees and a patch of chest high nettles, and then there were more buildings.

They came across a heavy white gate which they could not open, so they climbed over the top, rounded a corner, and found themselves in a cobbled yard. The sight before them rooted them both to the spot, neither could speak for several moments. Afterwards Lissa said she actually felt as though a bolt of electricity had struck her on the head, so sharp was the sensation that seized the back of her neck and spine. Cass recovered herself first and cried:

'Do you see what *I* see?'

'I don't believe it,' Lissa breathed.

They stared around them at a real stable-yard with buildings on three sides of a square. In front of them were seven loose-boxes with green stable doors, all securely bolted. At each side of the yard were long rooms with doors.

'It's a stable-yard,' Lissa said in a dazed voice. She walked slowly across the yard and touched the brick walls with her fingertips, half expecting the mirage to vanish. 'It's a stable-yard!' she repeated, her voice rising with excitement. 'And it belongs to us. Our very own stable-yard!'

'I don't believe it,' Cass squealed. She unbolted one of the doors and peered inside. A window high up on the far side let in a shaft of light, illuminating a floor of black stable-tiles, a steel hayrack, a manger, and rings in the walls for attaching headcollars. They opened each loose-box in turn, half hoping, though knowing it was impossible, that they might find a horse inside one of them. But in this dreamlike situation, who knew what amazing thing might happen next.

All the boxes were empty, of course, but at the end, in a room marked TACK, they did find a few old leather straps hanging on hooks a bit green with age, and an old, mildewed girth.

Beside the tack-room was a small yellow door which was locked. At the opposite side of the square was a feed-room, empty except for a couple of galvanised corn-bins, the remains of some bales of straw, and the sound of scuffling little feet.

'Is that a rat?' Cass asked anxiously.

'I don't know, but I'm not staying to find out!' Lissa said as they raced to the door.

Next to the feed-room was a tall, wide archway, wide enough for a carriage to pass through, and over the arch, a deep blue clock-face with gold hands which pointed to three o'clock. On the other side of the arch was another door to another building. They peered inside and saw in the half-light a wheelbarrow and garden tools stored there.

Lissa looked at her watch. 'We've had fifteen minutes,' she said.

'Oh, but we must just see where this track leads to,' Cass said urgently. They went on. On the left the tall hedge continued, and on the right a paddock fence separated the track from the vegetable garden, now a mass of weeds where giant cabbage stalks had gone to seed. Eventually they came to another large white gate in the hedge and there, before them, was a field which looked as though it had not been used or cut for years.

'It's just too good to be true,' Lissa said. They climbed on to the gate to feast their eyes on the sight before them. Already, in Lissa's imagination, a pony was grazing contentedly. Their very own field; a large one, too, if the distant hedgerow was the very end of it. An element of doubt struck them simultaneously – perhaps it did not belong to them at all. Perhaps it belonged to a neighbour-ing farmer. Yet all the gates led on to their own property.

The grassy track led further on through an orchard, but it was almost dark now and the girls knew their mother would be in a bad mood if they kept her waiting any longer, so, reluctantly, they turned back and found that by taking a sharp left at the shed they arrived back in the large courtyard behind the house itself.

As if by magic the two girls saw the house in a completely new light. As they walked through the kitchen door, the inside no longer seemed so dark, suddenly it was full of possibilities. What did it matter how or where they lived, just as long as they had their own stable-yard.

Two

Cass and Lissa entered the house again in blissfully high spirits. Mrs Tallis looked at them in a mixture of surprise and relief.

'Mummy, you're not going to believe this, but there's a real stable-yard out there, with stables and a tack-room and a feed-room and a field! An actual field!' Lissa said, the words tumbling out in her excitement.

'Oh, you found it. Well, I knew there was a bit of land and a few outbuildings . . .'

'It's a stable-yard! A real one with seven loose-boxes, and mangers and proper floors . . .'

'I can see it already, lots of beautiful heads looking over all the doors . . .' cried Cass. 'We'll have a palomino, and a grey . . .'

They were both talking at once in their eagerness. Mrs Tallis stared at them both in horror.

'But . . .' she tried to say.

'It's a real cobbled yard, with an archway leading out to the field. Oh, and a clock, only it doesn't work. And trees.'

'But we can hardly afford to feed ourselves, let alone a horse,' Mrs Tallis said.

'It won't cost much, only hay and feed in winter,' Cass assured her. 'Hardly anything in summer.'

'You can't say no, not when we've got everything, a stable, a field, and all of it free,' Lissa added urgently.

'Listen, girls,' Mrs Tallis said, very firmly. 'Maybe in two or three years, if you're still very keen and if we are a lot better off than we are now, then we might – *might* – invest in a pony. But not now. Be sensible. We moved here because we had no money. I'm at my wits end to know how to pay the rates, get all the repairs done and feed us all. So don't talk to me about ponies because it's quite out of the question.'

As she went on talking, her voice became less firm and more shaky. Another moment and it seemed disaster might strike them all – their mother might actually cry! Cassandra ran over to her mother and threw her arms around her.

'I'm sorry, Mummy. Don't worry.'

Lissa kicked at a spot on the floor with the toe of her wellington.

'I'd rather not eat at all if it meant we could have a pony.'

'Don't be silly. You would die.' Mrs Tallis said, her voice normal again.

'I don't care. I'd rather die.' And through her tears Lissa sobbed, 'I didn't want to leave the stables anyway. Oh, why does life have to be so horrible?'

'We will have a pony,' said Cassandra calmly. 'It will take a little time, that's all. We have to think up some plans for making money. If only I was older, I could start painting pictures to sell.'

The supper was getting cold when at last they came to eat it, but no one cared.

The next morning, Lissa woke suddenly with a sense of something wonderful happening, even before she opened her eyes. For a few moments she did not know what it was, and then she remembered the new stable-yard. Immediately her eyes opened and she bounced up. The bedclothes had not moved in the night, which meant she must have slept soundly.

From the kitchen came the clatter of plates and cutlery.

'Cass. Wake up.'

Cass opened her eyes and stared blankly at the strange, chaotic room. Then she, too, remembered. The two girls grinned at one another. Mrs Tallis appeared in the door-way, saying; 'Come on, it's late; it's after 10 o'clock and we've got a lot to do.'

Ginny was still sleeping so they woke her and ate breakfast round the coffee-table.

'We'll start cleaning out the yard this morning, shall we?' Cass suggested hopefully.

'No,' said her mother. 'We'll start cleaning out the house. I want the kitchen in a fit state to do some cooking. Tomorrow we'll go into town for some paint.'

'Are we going to paint the whole house?' asked Lissa, rather horrified.

'We don't have to do it all at once, as long as it's clean, that's the main thing; and I don't know if the curtains are going to fit . . .'

Lissa wasn't listening. All she could think of was their moment of discovery when they walked into the stable-yard the night before, and how long it might be before there would be a head or two peering over the door, calling to them every morning. She was trembling with excitement.

After breakfast, Cass and Lissa washed the dishes while their mother helped Ginny to find her shoes. Before starting work they slipped out for a quick look at the stables again, just to make sure they were really there and not just a dream.

'I wonder what's behind the yellow door,' said Cass, but Mrs Tallis was calling and there was no more time to think about it. The rest of the day was spent in cleaning, so that by night-time they were almost too tired to eat.

The next morning they made their first visit to the nearest town. It was a beautiful drive, and this time, with the clear blue sky above, they could see the sharp outline of distant hills and forests, and magnificent scenery in all directions. Several times they passed a group of horses in the fields, and each time the girls bounced up and down, crying 'Look! Look! Look!' until Mrs Tallis had to tell them to be still or the car would fall apart. The heathland was just made for riding, with wide gallops stretching for miles amid huge bands of heather, up hill and down. Even Mrs Tallis stopped frowning for a while.

It was a perfect day. Suddenly, after months of gloom, when it seemed that only bad things were going to happen for the rest of their lives, they could all breath free again, and the future was full of promising happenings. Every turn in the road brought something new to see, and a different landscape. Deep pink heather covered the hills for miles, contrasted with the charcoal remains of last year's fires, and the pale green of baby ferns pushing up through the sandy soil.

'We've come here at the best possible time,' Mrs Tallis remarked, 'with the whole summer ahead of us.'

'We could grow our own food, maybe then we wouldn't have to buy so much,' Lissa suggested. 'We saw a garden at the back with old cabbages and things.'

'Perhaps we could borrow a tractor from someone to dig it up,' added Cass. 'It was smothered in weeds.'

'I could get some seeds,' said Mrs Tallis, 'although when we'll find time to plant them, I don't know. It's a good idea, though.'

'What we really need to get everything growing is horse-manure,' said Lissa, and everyone laughed.

Mrs Tallis started singing a silly song they used to sing when Lissa was small and everyone joined in. Soon they were on the outskirts of the town. It was a pleasant little place, with friendly-looking shops dotted along the High Street. Along one side was a wide grass verge with a row of newly-planted young trees. Buds were bursting but it was too early to tell what kind of trees they were. When they had parked the car Mrs Tallis said the girls could explore for half an hour while she shopped for food as she wanted to concentrate without children under her feet.

There was a china shop next to the supermarket with small figures of horses and cats and other animals and they wasted a pleasant ten minutes there before moving on to a boutique where there were some pretty summer skirts and tee-shirts on display. When they had decided what they would buy if they had the money, they moved on past a hardwear shop and a baker's, and then turned a corner into a little side street. It was at that fateful moment that Lissa and Cassandra noticed the saddler's shop. Lissa said afterwards that it was definitely fate that had led them to the spot. They both stared in ecstasy at the bits and stirrups and jodhpurs and boots and horse blankets on display; curry combs, hoof picks, everything they could possibly want. Enough items to supply birthday presents for the next two hundred years, as Cass remarked.

'Let's go in.'

'Mummy won't know where we are.'

'We can keep a look out for her. Ginny can wait outside. Ginny, stay!' she said, as if to a dog.

Ginny's face puckered up as if to cry. 'I want to come,' she wailed.

'Oh, all right. But stay at the door and keep watch for Mummy.'

A loud bell rang as they pushed open the door of the saddler's. Inside it was quite dark, with piles of leather straps and clinking ironware hanging on every possible hook. Haynets, girths, leathers; the smell was heavenly.

'Can I help you, young ladies?' said a voice from the back. The saddler himself was busy repairing a broken rein, his eyes unnaturally close to his work. Lissa thought he needed more light to work by.

'No, thank you, not today,' Cassandra said awkwardly. 'We just wanted to look . . . if that's all right.'

'Help yourself, then,' he said cheerfully.

'You see, we haven't actually got our pony yet. But we will soon.'

'Ah, I see . . . Well, you'll find some of those on the wall,' said the man as he worked. The girls turned in amazement, expecting to see a selection of ponies strung up on the wall between the saddles and bridles. Instead, half relieved and half disappointed, they found a notice board with 'For Sale' cards on it. There were several:

16 hh iron-grey gelding. Good to shoe, box, clip.
Not novice ride.

12 hh palomino mare, 8 years, 100% no vices.

14.2 hh gelding, brilliant all rounder. Affiliated . . .

The list went on through horse-boxes for sale and

liveries available. And then, right at the bottom was a card that jumped right out and held their eyes, until, after some time, Lissa was aware that she had stopped breathing, and she had to breathe fast to catch up. It read:

FOR SALE OR LOAN
13.2 grey part Welsh Mountain mare
9 years, quiet to catch, shoe, box etc.
Kind home only. £450.

Lissa and Cass read it over and over again and looked at each other. They read it again. Was it possible to loan a pony? They wanted to ask the saddler, but he was buried in his work again and appeared to have forgotten them. Lissa, however, was staring at him so intently that he seemed to feel her eyes boring into him and looked up.

'Er, excuse me,' she said, 'but this card, the one at the bottom, it says "for sale or loan" – does that mean borrow? Without having to pay for it?' She felt her face grow hot and red as she spoke, knowing that her words gave them away.

'Ah, that's Mrs Beech's mare. Always comes to me for her bits and pieces. Her daughter's gone away to school, and anyways I reckon that one is a bit small for her now. Yes, I think she's put it on loan. Why, have you got somewhere to keep it?'

'We've got a most beautiful stable-yard,' cried Lissa, 'and our own field. We've just moved to White Trees Farm, and there are seven loose-boxes and a tack-room.'

'I know the place. Old Tom's had to go off to his sister's, hasn't he? Let it go a bit too, I shouldn't wonder. He couldn't do much with his arthritis. Well, you've got your work cut out there. It used to be a nice little place though. They kept hunters there when the Colonel was alive. About eight or nine acres, too.'

'Eight or nine acres? Really?' Lissa said in astonishment.

'Do you think she might let us have the pony?' asked Cass desperately.

'Well, now, there's no harm in asking, is there? That's what the advert's for.'

'Please, do you have a pen or something we could write with?' Cass persisted.

The very amiable saddler put down his work and took a pencil out of his top pocket, and on the back of a leaflet advertising a local gymkhana he copied down all the details that were on the card.

Then the doorbell rang again and Mrs Tallis came in:

'There you are! I've been looking everywhere.'

'Ginny was supposed to look out for you. Mummy, look . . .'

'Oh no!'

'It's on loan, look. A grey part Welsh Mountain, to borrow, free!' Cass went on, oblivious to her mother's look of horror.

'Thank you very much indeed for your help,' Lissa said hastily to the saddler, taking the paper from his hand. 'We have to go now.' She opened the door and dragged her mother out before the impending explosion.

Cassandra had a look of stony determination on her face. Nothing, but *nothing*, could come between them and this miracle. Their luck was at last changing, surely her mother would see that?

Three

'I'm sorry, girls. It's out of the question,' said Mrs Tallis when they were back in the car. 'I've got all kinds of expenses. You just don't understand.'

'But it won't cost anything all summer,' said Lissa. 'Ponies live on grass, and we've got plenty.'

'And what about shoes?'

'Well, apart from shoes . . . and we don't need to do much roadwork. We could just get her shod in front.'

'And what happens when winter comes?'

'We'll make some money by then, somehow,' Cass put in. 'If the worst happens we'll have to send her back. But at least we'll have had the summer.'

'That is not fair,' Mrs Tallis retorted. 'You cannot expect someone else to take her on just when it gets expensive. Besides, you know quite well you won't want to send her back.'

This was true.

'We'll find the money for feed from somewhere.'

'Oh, you think you'll find some tucked up the chimney or buried in the garden? Be sensible. I know how much you want this pony but it isn't possible. Not now. Maybe in a couple of years.'

'It won't be any different,' Lissa cried. 'It's never going to be any different.' Tears started to course down her cheeks and make dark patches on her pale blue tee-shirt.

'I'm beginning to wish we'd never come here!' her mother cried in despair.

'This pony is sent from heaven, we're meant to have it. We just have to think out how, that's all,' said Cass in her positive voice. 'Suppose we let rooms?'

'Nonsense, the place isn't fit to live in ourselves, let alone someone else pay to live there.' But her mother did not speak in so positive a tone.

Everyone was silent for a while, and Cassandra's idea, which had just dropped from nowhere, slowly took root in all their minds and grew into a scheme.

Finally, Mrs Tallis said, 'We'll think about it, but it will take time.'

Lissa gave a squeal of relief. She saw a chink of light in the darkness of the tunnel, a chink she could work on until it became a route.

'We haven't got time,' said Cass. 'Someone else may get the pony first. It may have gone already.' The two girls looked at each other in horror. Their mother glanced briefly from the road ahead and looked at their shining faces, a mixture of desperation and ecstatic joy.

'It will take long enough to get an advert in the paper,' she mused, 'then it will mean waiting for replies, interviewing people.'

'So we really ought to send the advert off today?' suggested Cass hopefully.

'We'll have to see if it's possible first. After all, even the bathroom is in a pretty bad state, and having to share it as well . . . we won't be able to ask very much.'

'There's some kind of room at the stables,' said Lissa. 'We haven't seen it yet because the door was locked.'

'I remember your grandfather saying something

about a gardener's cottage, but judging by the state of the house that will be even worse. It might be years since anyone has lived there.'

The drive home seemed to take twice as long as the drive to town, so anxious were they to get back, and the girls fidgeted impatiently in the back of the car.

Even before the car was unloaded, they were racing for the stairs to see if their scheme was possible, all three children shrieking at the tops of their voices. Ideas were flowing thick and fast, most of them wildly impractical as the cost of carrying them out far outweighed any benefits in the shape of rent money. It was not hopeful. The main bedroom was the most attractive to let as a bed-sitter and it had the best view, apart from the attic, but Mrs Tallis pointed out a very large patch of damp below the window which needed the attention of a builder. The two other bedrooms, both with damp patches on the ceiling where the roof let in the rain, would need to be seen by a plasterer; the attic, although of a good size, had rot in one corner and needed new floorboards. Mrs Tallis said no one could possibly live there until the work was done. They were sunk in gloom for a few minutes until Cass suggested:

'Let's go and look at the gardener's cottage.'

So Mrs Tallis collected the big bunch of keys from the kitchen and patiently traipsed with them through the gap in the hedge and into the yard.

'Look, Mother,' said Lissa. 'There's the tack-room, and that's the feed-room over there. And just look at the size of the loose-boxes; aren't they lovely?'

'It's very nice,' Mrs Tallis replied, surprised. 'It seems to be in better condition than the house. Obviously it shows how much more they used to think of their animals.'

'Here's the door,' said Cass.

After several attempts the right key was found and the yellow door swung open. Opposite was a small sitting-room with a window overlooking the paddock, and an open staircase leading up the inside wall to the floor above. Below the staircase was a door to a small kitchen, bare except for a gas stove and a sink unit, which was modern and clean apart from a layer of dust.

'It looks to me as though the tenant lived over here,' said Mrs Tallis, 'which would account for the appalling state of the house.'

Up the stairs they went and found themselves in a large room with windows on two sides. Beyond it was a small bathroom which Lissa said must be over the tack-room. There was a fireplace in the main room, obviously well used from the smoky appearance of the walls. Mrs Tallis went round testing the floorboards and checking that the windows were in working order. There was wallpaper on the walls, a little old-fashioned but in good repair.

'What do you think?' asked Cass. 'This would do, wouldn't it, Mummy?'

'I don't see why not. I should think whoever lived here must have looked after the place very well; in fact I would be tempted to move in here myself . . .'

'Oh, no, Mummy!'

' . . . if we didn't need the money.'

'We can do it, then?'

'I think we could make this a very cosy place indeed. It's a dear little cottage,' Mrs Tallis said.

'Oh, wow!' Cass and Lissa were dancing round in delight.

'I wish we could have it for a playhouse,' said Ginny.

'I'll hate horrid strangers living here.'

'We'll have to give it some decent furniture,' said Mrs Tallis, 'and I'll have to sort out some curtains. I think we ought to paper over these walls, which means another trip into town, I suppose.'

'We could put the advertisement in today, couldn't we?' asked Lissa.

'I suppose so,' replied her mother. 'It could well take a week before it goes into the paper, and we should be ready before then.'

'And could we *please* phone up about the pony, do you think?' Cass said urgently.

'Give me a couple of days to think about it.'

'But we might lose it,' wailed Lissa.

'There will be other ponies.'

'There won't be other ponies. Not free.'

'Perhaps she won't let you have it,' Mrs Tallis said. 'She might want it to go to a home where there are other ponies for company, or where people are more experienced in looking after them.'

'We've been helping at the stables for nearly two years, Mummy. We *can* look after it, really we can,' Cass insisted.

'Well, I suppose we could see what she says, although I don't feel at all ready for such a responsibility.'

After that there was no rest for Mrs Tallis until she picked up the receiver and called the number written on the back of the gymkhana leaflet. There was no reply. Cass and Lissa couldn't believe it. They took it in turns to keep trying all afternoon, but Mrs Beech was not at home. The rest of the day was spent in washing down paintwork, cleaning sinks and basins, sweeping floors, and making the cottage as fit to live in as possible. By night-time they were all exhausted again.

In the morning Mrs Tallis was persuaded to try the number again, and this time she spoke to Mrs Beech. The children watched her face, hoping to read what was being said in her expression. Lissa felt her mother did not really sound enthusiastic, and that perhaps Mrs Beech would think they were not interested enough to take the very best care of her pony. Both Cass and Lissa knew, that if they were entrusted with this pony, they would devote every minute of every day to her welfare and guard her with their lives.

'Mrs Beech? It's about your advertisement in the saddler's shop . . . that's right. So it hasn't gone yet? My name is Victoria Tallis, we have just moved into White Trees Farm. You know it? Yes, oh did he? How interesting. I saw it some years ago, when Mr Carter first moved in, and it looked quite nice then. I must say I was very disappointed at the . . . did you? Yes, the stables are very nice. Well, I don't know a lot about ponies myself, but the girls are very keen, and they have been working at some stables for almost a couple of years. Lissa's eleven, and Cass is ten. They've never had a pony but they know a little about looking after it . . .'

'More than a little!' hissed Cass indignantly. Lissa buried her head in her hands; the suspense was more than she could bear.

'Yes, of course,' Mrs Tallis continued. 'When would you like to come over? Thursday will be fine. About eleven o'clock. Thank you . . . I look forward to meeting you, too. No, we don't have any tack. Until Thursday. Thank you. Goodbye.' Their mother came off the phone looking thoughtful.

'Thursday!' Cass cried. 'Why not tomorrow?'

33

'Mrs Beech is busy tomorrow, she's going to a show with one of her hunters,' Mrs Tallis explained. 'But she asked if we had our own tack, or if we would be buying any. It's a little awkward really, but I think she might lend us some until we can buy it. That is, if she likes the look of us.'

'Oh, she must, surely,' Cass said anxiously.

'At least the pony hasn't gone to anyone else yet.'

'We need to sweep out a loose-box and check the paddock to make sure there are no loose rails or poisonous weeds,' Lissa said.

'Would you know them if you saw them?' asked her mother.

'I think so. Mrs Harrison used to point them out, and it's in our book on horse ailments.'

'Well, you can do all that tomorrow. After I've sorted out the advertisement – we'll have to go into town again. Even if you don't get the pony, I still think letting the cottage is a very good idea.'

'If we have a pony, can I ride it?' asked Ginny.

'Of course,' replied her mother. 'The girls will teach you.'

Cass suddenly jumped up and down and yelled, 'I can't stand it! I can't stand having to wait until Thursday!'

So many things could go wrong. They wanted to go and check the field now to make sure everything was all right. Suppose there was some old machinery left in the grass, and Mrs Beech saw it and said that they were far too irresponsible to have the care of a pony. Or suppose she let them have the pony and it hurt itself in some way. Perhaps it would take hours to check the field properly . . .

There was nothing they could do but wait. Mrs Tallis

34

wrote out an advertisement for the local newspaper and phoned it in. It read: *Secluded cottage available, 2 rooms, kitchen and bathroom. £50.00 per week. Telephone* . . .

After that they got ready for another trip into the town, which, as Cass said, would use up another two hours while they were waiting for Thursday to come. Once in the town, they went straight to the wallpaper shop to browse among the papers on display, and discovered that they each had different ideas about the kind of thing they were looking for. Mrs Tallis said it was a cottage and should therefore have a simple pattern with a tiny print all over and frilly curtains to match. Lissa said that would make it look like a doll's-house, and they ought to get something modern, like a plain hessian paper, in case someone like a scientist wanted to rent it, but Mrs Tallis said it would be too expensive; and after almost an hour of discussion the children got bored and said they would go and say hello to their friend the saddler.

Halfway along the High Street, Lissa stopped and cried, 'Oh! Look! The baby trees, somebody has been attacking them.'

Cass walked back to where she stood. Two of the newly-planted young trees that they had admired on their first visit to the town now drooped forlornly, with three of their lower limbs fractured at a sharp angle, showing the freshly-splintered white wood inside.

'Can we mend it, do you think?' Lissa asked. 'Have you got any string?'

'I've got some baling twine in my pocket,' Cass replied, 'but we need something to put round the bark so the string doesn't cut in. Ginny, have you got a hanky?'

'Yes, but it's my Peter Rabbit one and you can't have it!' Ginny said firmly.

'Ginny, the tree's life is at stake,' Lissa pleaded.

'You can't have it,' Ginny repeated.

'Well, we'll have to manage,' said Lissa.

Carefully they tore a tissue into strips, and while Cass held the tattered branches straight Lissa gently bound them with the material and then wound the string around to hold it firm. When both trees were finished they stood back to admire their work, and Lissa gave the slim trunk a final stroke.

'Goodbye, trees. We'll come and see you again.'

'Can they hear you?' asked Ginny.

'Of course they can.'

'They haven't got any ears.'

'They can't speak either, but they can feel, and they know what is going on.'

'How do you know?'

'I know.'

As they passed another young tree, Ginny turned her head and said, 'We're going to have a new pony.'

The young branches waved up and down, though there was no wind. Ginny's eyes grew round with wonder. 'Did it hear me?' she asked.

'Of course,' Lissa assured her, and then Ginny wanted to speak to every tree, until Cass had to tell her firmly:

'That's enough, or there won't be time to get to the saddler.'

He was working in the same place as before, sitting at the back of his dark little shop, working on some leather. Mrs Beech's card was still on the wall and, after saying hello, Cass told him that they were probably going to have the pony and perhaps the card could come down now.

'Well, I'm pleased to hear that,' he replied. 'She's a

nice little mare. I seem to remember she jumps quite well. But I'd better leave the card there till Mrs Beech says it's to come down, since she's paid for it. What will you do about a saddle?'

'She's got her own tack,' Cass replied, and said nothing about it not being paid for, although she felt he was the kind of friend that you could tell anything, and he wouldn't blame you.

They watched him work for a while, and it seemed no time at all before there was a tap on the window and Mrs Tallis was waiting.

As soon as they got home, Cass and Lissa made tea and sandwiches for lunch while Mrs Tallis changed her clothes and started work on the ceilings of the cottage. Cass and Lissa worked on the doors and window frames, and by the end of the day it was looking brighter. They stood looking at their handiwork for a few minutes, then they all trailed sleepily back to the house for supper. Mrs Tallis told everyone to go to bed early as they were all working so hard.

Lissa found the alarm clock, set it for seven o'clock, and put it under her pillow, hoping it would not wake her mother so early.

Four

It seemed as if she had slept for only half an hour when the shrill bell warbled under her pillow. Lissa was so tired that she was tempted to ignore it and just carry on sleeping, but then she remembered that Mrs Beech was coming tomorrow. She crept out of bed and gently pushed Cass until she woke.

'Come on, we've got to check the field,' Lissa whispered to her.

Together they took their clothes and crept out to the kitchen to dress so that they would not wake their mother and Ginny. There was a chill in the house at that early hour, as they still had no heating, and outside the grass glistened with dew.

'Oh, good grief, I'm so tired,' Cassandra yawned.

'Me too. But don't think about it. We'll go round the field first,' said Lissa, 'because we won't need the stable just now and the field is more important.'

Cass agreed.

The sun was just above the trees and the grass was steaming. Their jeans were still damp from washing walls, and felt stiff and uncomfortable, but in their excitement they hardly noticed.

They opened the paddock gate with some difficulty. The hinges were rather rusty and Cass decided that when her mother woke up she would ask her where the oil was and try to fix it. The field was enormous – Lissa estimated about three acres, it was certainly easily the size of three football pitches, she thought. They made their way round the outside and found that two sides were bordered by hawthorn and hazels which had run completely wild, but made such a solid hedge that they would certainly prevent a pony from escaping. A third side, belonging to a neighbour, was well trimmed, and the fourth, bordering on their own garden, was a paddock fence. A couple of rails were broken but Cass thought she could fix them with a hammer and some nails.

In one corner stood a group of three giant chestnut trees, their branches trailing almost to the ground on one side. It was possible to walk right inside and stand in the large hollow where hardly any grass grew in the thick carpet of fallen leaves and nutshells. They crossed and recrossed the field, looking for any object that might harm a pony, but fortunately could find nothing.

After that they began work on the stable. They chose the loose-box furthest away from the cottage, so the pony would not disturb their new tenant, and washed down the walls and floor with a broom and some brushes which they found in the shed opposite the feed-room. Then they spread some straw over the floor, setting up and smoothing the sides as they had been taught at the stables. By now it was well past eight o'clock and they decided it was all right to wake their mother.

Lissa put the kettle on and made a pot of tea while Cass searched for tools among the packing-cases. The noise woke Mrs Tallis.

'What on earth are you two doing up so early?' she asked.

'I'm actually looking for the nails and hammer,' Cass said. 'Mrs Beech is coming tomorrow, remember, and we found a couple of rails loose in the fence. We mustn't give her any excuse to say we can't have the pony.'

Her mother groaned and fell back on to her pillow. 'I'd forgotten. Oh, what made me agree to all this?' She sat up, though, as Lissa walked in carrying the steaming mug of tea. 'What a nice surprise. Thank you,' she said.

'Where's the hammer?' Cass persisted.

'I think you'll find all the tools in the box with the flowerpots on top, over there in the corner.'

'And the oil?'

'What's that for?'

'The hinges on the gate are a bit rusty,' Cass explained.

'That should be there as well. We'll get some rust remover next time we go into town. I've got to go over the car with it when I have time.'

Cass found what she was looking for and disappeared.

Lissa sat on the sofa to drink her tea, and suddenly felt quite sleepy. Also, her jeans were soaking wet and she wondered whether to change. Her mother decided for her and ordered her to put something else on at once, an old play-skirt would do to work in.

'How did you get so wet?' asked Mrs Tallis. 'I suppose Cass is in the same state?'

'Oh, yes,' Lissa said brightly, as if that halved her responsibility. 'We were washing down the stable.' She began to rummage for the rest of her clothes in the packing-cases while her mother went upstairs to wash and dress and, by the time she came down, the chaos in the living-room was twice as bad as before. For the first time since arriving at their new home, Mrs Tallis lost her temper.

'As if things aren't bad enough without you turning everything upside down. At least I had some idea where everything was before,' she said furiously.

'You said to put on my play-skirt, and I can't find it,' Lissa replied indignantly.

'All your summer clothes are in the blue suitcase with Cass's.'

'Oh, I forgot.'

Ginny woke up then, wailing, 'I'm tired.'

'We're all tired!' yelled her mother, and stomped into the kitchen, slamming the door behind her.

Lissa felt tears pricking her eyelids. Life was so unfair. How else could you find things except by looking? She tried to pack everything up where it was before, but somehow nothing would fit. Then she had an idea, and went upstairs to find the empty wardrobes. They were ranged side by side in the big bedroom, so she went back and collected armfuls of her and Cassandra's clothes and after several journeys everything was beautifully hung where it could be found. After that she started on her mother's things, and finally Ginny's. Three empty cases were stowed away in the attic and an entire packing-case emptied by the time breakfast was ready, and all the bedclothes were neatly folded. At that moment, Cass came back, looking hot and untidy and nursing a badly-bruised thumb.

'I think that's fixed for now,' she said cheerfully.

When Mrs Tallis returned to the living-room, she put her arms round Lissa and gave her a hug without speaking. Suddenly Lissa felt better, she hated to quarrel with anyone, and most especially with her mother. Soon they were ready to continue work, though Lissa wondered how they would ever manage to get through another whole day, particularly when she felt so tired to begin with. However, once they started she soon forgot how tired she was and even began to enjoy herself, although Ginny would keep forgetting about wet paint and insisted on walking into doorways, leaving behind little patches of pink wool from her jumper. Every time this happened Cass or Lissa would give a yell of rage, while Mrs Tallis wailed for the destruction of the jumper.

After a couple of hours the fun wore off, and all Lissa could think about was what they could say to Mrs Beech the next day to convince her that she should let them have the pony. She began to feel sick with anxiety. Finally she started to make mistakes and spill things, so Mrs Tallis became exasperated and sent both girls off to play. They climbed up into a chestnut tree and tried to imagine what it would be like to have a pony grazing down below.

Early the next morning, they were up and dressed in their jodhpurs and clean jumpers and were stationed at the attic window where they could see the road in the distance crossing the heathland, and the cars like little ants on the skyline. If Mrs Beech came the other way, they could see the curve in the road beyond the driveway. There was still an hour to go. The hands on Lissa's watch crawled slowly round; ten-fifteen, ten-twenty, ten-thirty . . . five to eleven. Several cars passed at intervals, and each time the girls held their breath to hear if one should slow down and turn in. Eleven o'clock came and went, but no Mrs Beech. A quarter past, still no sign, and they were starting to give up hope.

'I knew it was too good to be true,' Cass remarked, and as she did so a small blue Renault came sailing across the hill, down to White Trees Farm, slowing at the last minute with a screech of brakes, and swung into the gateway. Lissa and Cass raced down the stairs and arrived at the open front door just as Mrs Beech came to a stop.

'Hello!' she said, in a rather booming voice. 'Are you the Tallis girls?' She was tall and wiry, wispy grey hair framing a brown, weatherbeaten face with amazingly sharp blue eyes. She wore a duffel coat over an old checked skirt.

'Yes,' they replied. 'Are you Mrs Beech?'

'How do you do.' She shook hands formally. 'Where's your mother?'

Lissa had a sudden vision of her mother in the cottage, with her hands and hair covered in paint, and said, 'I'll go and tell her you're here.' She ran on ahead through the hedge while Cass took Mrs Beech round the long way, through the arch into the yard.

'Here we are,' said Cass. 'We thought this box would be a nice one. And there's the feed store, and the tack-room is over there.' She waved her arms as she spoke, then opened the half-door so that Mrs Beech could see inside.

'Nice little yard,' said Mrs Beech, looking round appreciatively. 'So you've done a bit of riding, have you?'

'Oh, yes. We've been riding for two years. We've been in for some shows, too.'

'And you've been helping to look after ponies as well?'

'Where we used to live we were at the stables every evening and weekend, doing everything, mucking-out, grooming, cleaning tack . . .'

'And what if the pony gets ill?' Mrs Beech asked.

'Well, we'd have to call a vet, I suppose,' said Cass, her face going red because she knew vets cost quite a lot of money.

'I should expect you to let me know immediately if

43

Sara was ill,' Mrs Beech said severely.

'Yes, of course,' Cass replied, rather meekly.

Mrs Tallis came out then, looking reasonably free of paint, with Lissa dancing at her heels like a puppy.

Mrs Beech shook hands, and they started talking about all kinds of things, farms and houses and land and decorating, and lettuces, herb gardens, kitchens ... but not ponies. Lissa thought she was going to die. How could they do this? Finally, Mrs Beech suggested they look at the paddock. They led her down the overgrown track to the big white gate and showed her the field. She seemed pleased that it was such a nice, large field, and even more so when Mrs Tallis told her that beyond it were two more large fields that were used by a neighbouring farmer at the moment.

Then Mrs Beech started talking about the Colonel who used to live at White Trees Farm years ago, when the yard was full of hunters. 'It was a splendid garden then,' she said, 'with a pond in the front and some very fine shrubs. The lawn was like a bowling-green. Of course, you know the grass is too long?' she added suddenly, turning back to the field. 'Horses can get laminitis when the grass is too long, especially at this time of year when it's getting rich.'

'Yes, of course,' both girls said at once, and Lissa wondered where their book on horse ailments was packed, so that they could read up about it.

'What can we do about that?' their mother asked.

'Get it cut down a bit. Perhaps Mr Crawford could help you out. He's just next door and a very helpful sort of man; or if he hasn't got time I could send John over.'

'John?'

'My man. He looks after our place, and the ponies

44

as well. He wouldn't mind coming over, but give Mr Crawford a ring first.'

'We'll certainly see to that. I'll ask Mr Crawford today,' said Mrs Tallis. 'Apart from that, what do you think?'

'Oh, I think Sara would be in clover here,' said Mrs Beech, smiling. 'I know my daughter would be glad to know her pony has such a good home. But I do want to know if anything goes wrong, or if she gets ill. And you do understand that if someone should want to buy her, I might have to ask for her back again?'

'Yes, of course,' said Mrs Tallis. 'I suppose the next thing is for the girls to try her out and make sure they can manage her.'

'I certainly would like to see them ride her, but they won't have any trouble with Sara. Gentle as a lamb; your youngster there could manage her,' Mrs Beech said pointing to Ginny. 'But she's willing, too. A little gem of a pony.'

Lissa suddenly remembered about tack, and gave her mother a nudge.

'What is it?' asked Mrs Tallis. Lissa blushed.

'Ask about the tack,' she whispered.

'Oh, yes!' She turned back to Mrs Beech. 'You did mention a saddle and bridle?'

'Ah,' Mrs Beech looked thoughtful. 'You don't have any tack?'

'Not yet.'

'Is there any chance of you getting some? I don't really want to let the tack go – it can so easily get damaged.'

'In time,' said Mrs Tallis, 'but not immediately. Unless we could borrow it and pay you later. That is if you are prepared to sell it.'

'I don't mind doing that. It's too small for the others,

and it does fit her nicely. Let me see, it's not a new saddle, but it's in quite nice condition. How about £100 all in?'

Their mother's face went pale. Mrs Beech added, 'You can have her rug as well for that.'

'It will have to be a bit later on,' Mrs Tallis murmured faintly.

Lissa was thinking: If we let the cottage a week from now, we could have £100 in three weeks' time.

'I'm not in a hurry – say a month's time,' said Mrs Beech. Lissa was grinning from ear to ear. Mrs Beech went on, 'So, it's just a matter of the girls coming over to try her. How about the weekend?'

Lissa thought her heart would burst. 'Can't we see her sooner?' she blurted out.

'Oh, yes, *please*,' Cass implored.

Mrs Beech laughed. 'Well, let's see. I'm a bit tied up this afternoon, but if you'd like to come over about five, I should be back by then.'

'If you'd rather make it the weekend . . .' Mrs Tallis began.

'No, we'd better not keep them waiting. I know what these girls are like,' Mrs Beech replied.

'Five it is then, Would you like some coffee?'

'No, no, I'm on my way into town. Very nice to meet you all. I'm sure you'll get on famously with Sara.' Then she was in her little blue Renault and shooting away up the hill again.

Mrs Tallis passed a weary hand over her brow and sighed. 'Now, where on earth will we get £100 in a month's time?'

'From letting the cottage,' Lissa cried. 'It's all working out beautifully. Let's ring Mr Crawford right away.'

After a chat on the phone with Mr Crawford, their

next-door neighbour, whose house was at the end of a tiny lane on the other side of the field, he agreed to send one of his men round with a machine to trim the grass down. Mrs Tallis asked anxiously how much he would charge them. He replied that he would do it instead of paying the month's rent on the two fields which, he informed her, was £60 a month. Also, Mrs Crawford was wanting to speak to her; she had been waiting for a chance to get acquainted and suggested that Mrs Tallis go round to see her for a cup of coffee.

Mrs Tallis came off the phone looking extremely happy. After lunch, she decided on a rest. They were too excited to work, anyway. The minute-hand crawled round the clock so slowly they had to keep listening to check that it was still going.

'Can I ride the new pony today?' Ginny asked.

'No,' said Cass. 'You've never ridden before, and we don't want to give Mrs Beech any excuse to change her mind. I wonder what she'll expect us to do. Do you think she'll want to see us jump?'

'I think we should just do a bit of schoolwork and ride her really quietly. We don't want Mrs Beech to think we're going to be racing her around, wearing her out,' Lissa replied.

'Just think, we'll be able to go out for a hack up on that wide track we saw over the downs. We could even take a picnic,' said Cass dreamily.

'Isn't it amazing? We're going to have a pony.' Lissa still could not quite believe it was happening.

'She's not really ours though, and just suppose Mrs Beech decides to sell her?'

'She won't, not for ages anyway. And by the time she does perhaps we might be able to buy her.' Lissa said

47

confidently. 'I really feel as if our luck has changed. Perhaps this is a lucky house after all.'

'I hope so,' Cass was less sure. 'Anyway, we haven't got her yet.'

At five o'clock they drove the battered old Morris between high wrought-iron gates and up a gravelled drive between some rhododendron bushes not yet in bloom. Mrs Beech lived in a long, white bungalow with a wide brick porch, framed by the gnarled, grey trunk of some climbing plant which was just bursting into leaf. Mrs Tallis knocked on the studded oak door. A pair of golden retrievers came to greet them from the garden, wagging their tails and lifting their heads to be caressed.

Mrs Beech opened the door and, without any further preamble, led them straight to the small yard where, from a row of loose-boxes, a solitary grey head watched their approach with eagerness.

'The other horses are out in the daytime now,' Mrs Beech told them. She waved an arm at the girls. 'Bring her out, then.'

Cass and Lissa looked at each other, now slightly scared. Lissa was the one to move forward and unbolt the door. Sara was already tacked up, with her reins tucked under a stirrup leather, Lissa's hands were shaking slightly and her fingers fumbled to free the reins and lift them over the pony's head. Then she walked ahead out of the box and Sara followed obediently.

They all stood round, admiring the pretty grey head with the dark, charcoal coloured mane and points. Her coat was still a bit shaggy in places where her winter fur had not completely come away, but her mane and tail were full and bushy and very silky.

Lissa rubbed the soft whiskery nose, feeling that special

excitement she always felt when handling ponies, and in return Sara gave her a butt with her head that nearly knocked her off-balance.

'Let's take her round the paddock,' said Mrs Beech, leading the way. There was a sand school and a few jumps round the edge of the field. Lissa got up first, after remembering to tighten the girth, and then shortened the stirrups, feeling very self-conscious as she did so. She hoped Mrs Beech would not think her very inexperienced. Fortunately her mother was chatting away and Mrs Beech did not appear to be watching her, so Lissa stopped feeling nervous and started enjoying herself. It was glorious to be on top of a pony again and feel the lovely furry neck beneath her fingers. Sara's ears were pricked, obviously surprised by this unusual development.

'She hasn't had a lot of work lately since there's no one to ride her,' Mrs Beech was saying. 'She needs a bit of muscling up, so take it slowly for a few weeks, build her up gradually. Lots of walking and trotting.'

So no jumping! Lissa was partly relieved, partly disappointed. She walked and trotted Sara round the paddock, did a few circles and a figure of eight, and one short canter, then she pulled up and let Cass have a turn.

Sara was not as willing as she had expected. It took two or three sharp kicks to persuade her to move on, but that was probably because she was not fit.

'What do you think of her?' asked Mrs Beech.

'She's lovely,' said Lissa emphatically.

'You'll find she loves gymkhanas. She'll get much more lively when she loses that fat tummy and gets some muscle on her.'

'We'll take her for long walks,' Lissa said.

'Well, I take it you would like to have her, then?' Mrs

Beech turned to Mrs Tallis. Cass was still circling the paddock, an ecstatic grin on her face.

'Yes, I think so,' replied their mother.

'And you'll let me have the money for the tack in about a month?'

'If not before,' Mrs Tallis said.

Mrs Beech held out her hand and Mrs Tallis shook it. 'Let me know when the grass is cut and I'll arrange for John to bring her over in the trailer,' said Mrs Beech. 'It isn't far to ride, but there is a nasty main road to cross, so it's best to be on the safe side.'

'Come on, Cass,' her mother called eventually, when it seemed that Cass would carry on riding all night. Mrs Beech put Sara out with the other horses after taking off the tack and without waiting to move away, Sara's head went down and she began eating.

Five

'Why does everything have to be in straight rows?' Cassandra asked, holding a packet of lettuce seeds in her hand. 'Why can't we just plant them in a big square?'

'Because,' Lissa said. 'I don't know. It's just the way they do it, that's all. Do you think we've dug it deep enough?'

'It will have to be,' Cass replied. 'My back hurts from all this digging. You make the groove, and I'll sprinkle them in.' They worked in silence for the next few minutes until all the seeds were planted. 'What's next?' Cass asked.

'Nothing. We've finished. Mummy said to leave the tomatoes, because she wants to put them in the green-house . . . We haven't really done very much, have we?'

The two girls stood and looked at the square of rich, dark earth which had taken them almost two hours to dig. It was only a tiny corner of the garden.

'It's impossible to dig it all up,' Cass said. 'We need a tractor or something.'

Ginny appeared on the path beside them. 'Is that all you've done?' she said.

'I shall strangle you if you're not careful,' said Cass.

'I want my doll's-house, only it's in one of the packing-cases. Can you help me find it?'

'Where's Mummy?' asked Lissa.

'In the cottage, putting the paper up,' Ginny told her.

'Oh, all right, only you'll have to wait while I clean this earth off my hands,' Lissa said.

After a lot of searching, they found the packing-case with all Ginny's toys in it, and emptied the contents on to the bedroom floor where she could play to her heart's content without getting in the way. They left her with the portable radio playing, for company.

'Let's go and explore the rest of the garden,' suggested Cass. 'There are lots of useful things lying around.'

In the yard at the back was a kind of open barn, where a piece of old machinery was parked next to the firewood. On the left, joining the barn to the house, was the pretty, gabled shed which, if you passed right through it, brought you out just behind the arch to the stable-yard. Inside the shed were garden tools, two wheelbarrows, boxes of rusty old screws, hammers, a watering-can, hundreds of flowerpots in all shapes and sizes, and even an old bicycle with two flat tyres.

Beyond that was a wilderness of grass and overgrown shrubs. It might have been pretty once, but now it was difficult to find a pathway through the weeds. Further on, past the vegetable garden, was a mass of neglected trees with wild black branches bursting into leaf. This was the orchard. The wide, grassy track which ran down the side of the vegetable garden to the paddock continued through the orchard, finishing at the far end in another gate, completely covered over by hawthorn from the untrimmed hedge. Pushing aside the branches, the girls saw black and white cows grazing peacefully on well-tended pastureland.

'That must be one of our fields,' said Lissa. 'So they

must be Mr Crawford's cows. Aren't they lovely?' The nearest cows looked up and gazed at the girls with interest, then lowered their heads and carried on grazing.

'I wish he would hurry up and trim our grass. We could have had the pony today,' Cass said.

'Let's go and climb the chestnut trees,' Lissa suggested.

In the paddock, the three chestnuts stood in their corner like giant sentinels, giving perfect shelter from rain, wind or snow, the lower branches spreading a natural screen right down to touch the grass. They were not easy trees to climb; the massive, deeply-grooved branches were set far apart, further than their legs could reach but, by shinning up the outside screen, Lissa and Cass managed to achieve a position about a third of the way up.

'Look, you can see right over to the village at Chaseford!' said Cass. 'It won't be such a good view when the leaves are all out, though.'

'No, but it will be a marvellous hiding-place.' Lissa replied. 'Oh, I do love trees.' She spread her arms across the huge trunk and pressed her face into the rough bark, as if she could fuse with it, and let the pulse of the tree go right through her. She felt as if she could draw strength from the tree, and give back all of her own. It was the kind of fusing with nature that her father used to speak of, a kind of delightful friendship quite different from the sort you can have with people. Not a substitute, but very powerful in its own way.

Cass broke into her thoughts. 'We need a rope, so we can climb up here more easily. We could bring a picnic up here,' she suggested. 'Look, you can see the stable roof, the gutters need clearing out, there's grass growing in them.'

'We'll do it tomorrow. I don't feel like doing anything now,' Lissa said lazily.

Eventually they wandered back to the stable-yard. Most of the afternoon had gone, though it was still quite warm. They could hear their mother singing through the open windows of the cottage.

'I can't stand waiting,' Lissa moaned, looking over the door of the loose-box which they had prepared for Sara. 'Why can't that man come today? We could be riding now.'

'Hello, you two,' Mrs Tallis said, emerging from behind the yellow door. 'I've nearly finished the upstairs. Would you like to see?'

Inside, the cottage had taken on a completely new character. It was warm, welcoming, and extremely pretty. The new wallpaper blended perfectly, a small neat pattern which somehow made the room seem even larger. Everywhere the paintwork was gleaming where the final coat was almost dry. The bathroom walls were a soft rose pink to blend with the paper.

'It's a pity we can't afford a new carpet,' their mother said regretfully, 'but the one from my old bedroom will do. It's a sort of stone colour. Just the curtains to make now, and it's ready.'

'I wish we could live here. It's such a lovely place,' said Cass. The view was heavenly, clear across the fields to the distant skyline of blue and wooded hills. The may-blossom was bursting out in the hedgerows, and the misty white masses glowed in contrast with the rich green of the meadows.

'We'll soon get the house looking as good as this,' her mother said.

'When there's time, I think I'll do some painting,' said

Cass. 'In fact, I'd like to do this view before anyone moves in and we won't be able to see it any more.'

'Well, you'll have to do it today then, before I get the new curtains up, because I don't want them splashed with paint! Why don't you bring a chair over from the house, you can rest your drawing board on the window-sill. I painted it yesterday so it should be dry now.'

'I will,' Cass cried, quite carried away now by a flow of ideas, and she ran away to the house to look for her painting materials.

'Aren't you going to do a painting as well?' Mrs Tallis asked Lissa.

Lissa shrugged. 'I feel too restless. I don't think I would get very far with it. I can't stop thinking about the pony.'

'Well, you won't have long to wait now.'

'I won't really believe it until I see Sara's face looking over our gate. Anything could happen – Mrs Beech might change her mind.'

'I'm sure she won't. I expect Mr Crawford's man will be round tomorrow.'

In fact, Mr Crawford's man came a little later that day, just as they had given up any hope, and there were barely two hours of daylight left. He fairly flew round the field and by the time darkness fell, most of the work was done. He said he would leave the machine in their yard and promised to come back first thing in the morning to finish off.

Lissa wanted to ring Mrs Beech right away but her mother said no, they must wait until it was completely ready. At eight-thirty in the morning Greg was back again, and very soon the field was ready. Mrs Tallis gave him a slice of cake and some coffee and as he sat in the kitchen, laughing and joking, the girls thought him a very friendly sort of neighbour to have.

'You've got yourself a job here all right, putting this place in order again,' he said. 'Poor old Tom couldn't do much for himself the last year or so. I see the garden's gone to pieces as well.'

'We'll get it tidied up when the house is fit to live in,' said Mrs Tallis.

'Yes, I saw a few tiles loose up there. The trouble is, when the wind blows from the north, you get it straight across the heath. Well, if you want any help there, my brother's a good hand at roofing. He does any kind of repair.'

'That's nice to know,' she said warily. 'I'll be glad to have his name, but I'm afraid the roof will have to wait its turn.'

'Don't wait too long, missus, the damp can do a lot of harm. I'll tell him to give you a ring. You'll find him very reasonable. Well, thanks for the coffee.' Greg stood up and picked up his cap. He was so tall that his head nearly touched the ceiling, and the girls gasped in unison.

In the yard, he stood looking around in an amiable sort of way and asked, 'Does Tom's old cultivator still go?'

'Cultivator?' Mrs Tallis echoed blankly.

'Ay – the machine for digging up your cabbage patch.'

He sauntered over to where the machine was propped in a corner of the barn, turned a few knobs and pulled a handle. A harsh, grating noise followed, then a few splutters and it stopped. Greg tapped on the tank and said, 'You could try putting a bit of petrol in, but it doesn't sound too hopeful. It needs a good clean-up, and maybe

57

some new plugs, but it's worth a try.'

'I've given up any thought of trying to get the garden in order just yet,' Mrs Tallis said.

Greg shook his head. 'If you don't get the spuds in soon, missus, it'll be too late. Should've been in by now.'

'We've only been here just over a week,' she said faintly.

'Ah, well, first things first. Watch out for those window-frames, though, they'll start rotting if you don't get some paint on them,' he said cheerfully, and sauntered off down the driveway.

'Oh dear,' Mrs Tallis said, 'I am worried about the roof.'

'He's right, it's awfully wet up there,' Lissa said.

'Well, I suppose that's our next priority,' her mother sighed.

'Except for ringing Mrs Beech, she'll be waiting to hear from us,' said Lissa, feeling torn between guilt and desperation. Her mother suddenly looked very tired, but she went dutifully over to the phone and made the call. Mrs Beech said John would be over the next day with the trailer and she wished them luck.

Lissa and Cassandra danced round with joy, hugging each other. 'Tomorrow! Tomorrow! We're going to have a pony *at last*.'

Six

Mrs Tallis lay in a crumpled heap on the sofa, her feet on the coffee-table.

'If one of us did that, you'd be raging mad!' Cass exclaimed, with some indignation.

'I'm allowed. I'm a mother. One of you go and make some coffee before we start work again.' She smiled in a sceptical way as they both headed for the kitchen at once and collided in the doorway. 'I suppose I can expect help for another half-day at least until this pony arrives and carries you off to another planet.'

Wide-eyed, Cass said, 'But we're always helpful, Mummy.'

As she sipped her coffee, Mrs Tallis glanced around her at the smoky ceiling and mildewed walls, and said, 'This is the next room to be done. What colour shall we do it?'

Cass and Lissa looked at each other and smiled. 'You decide,' Cass said. 'You always do.'

Then, out of the blue, Ginny said, 'Mummy, could we have a piano?'

'A what?'

'Rosie Stewart's got a piano. She's taking her Grade I soon.'

'But you're only six.'

'Rosie Stewart says that's the best age to start.'

'I thought you didn't like Rosie Stewart.'

'No, but I like pianos.'

'And since you'll probably never see your old school again, you will probably never see Rosie Stewart again.'

'But can we?' Ginny persisted.

'Ginny, darling, your timing is impeccable. Here's me worrying about the roof, your sisters hustling for a pony, and now suddenly you want a piano.'

'I've wanted one for ages.'

'You never said so.'

'I knew we couldn't have one,' said Ginny.

'We still can't,' her mother replied. 'Not right now. But if you really want one, we'll see. Later on.'

'How much later?'

'Who knows. Now, be a good girl and don't bother me about it right now. I've got the curtains to make, and then we start on this room. Can you two help me move the dining-table over here near the plug, then I can set up the sewing-machine.'

Soon Mrs Tallis was engrossed in measuring and cutting material and wanted to be left alone. Cass wanted to finish her painting so Lissa got out some gardening tools and began clearing the weeds from the stable-yard. It would all help to make the cottage more attractive, she told Cass.

Lunch was over, and the whole afternoon dragged by.

'Why do adults always do things at the last possible moment?' Lissa moaned to Cass. 'When I'm grown up I shall never keep children waiting. I shall always do everything immediately.'

'You can't do everything immediately,' Cass pointed out logically.

The picture was coming along well; Cass had captured the ghostly whiteness of the bushes against the deep blue of the sky, and the tangle of black branches below them. There were a few homes dotted on the landscape, a Jacobean mansion, a white farm building, and the red roofs of cottages.

'It's really good,' Lissa said in surprise on her fourth visit. She kept wandering up to watch Cass work, then getting bored and going back to her weeding. 'You really are getting better, Cass. Perhaps you ought to be an artist.'

'I'm going to be a showjumping rider,' Cass replied.

'Perhaps you could do both,' Lissa suggested. 'I wish I could paint like that.'

'You could if you practised.'

'I get bored. I like painting horses, though.'

'Why don't you just paint horses, then?'

'We could paint Sara.'

'Why don't they hurry up? Mrs Beech did say this afternoon, didn't she?'

'Yes . . . Listen.'

At that very moment they heard the sound of heavy wheels grinding up the drive. With a whoop of delight they leapt down the stairs and rushed round to the front of the house.

A pony could be led through the gate in the hedge, but the trailer had to follow the drive right round to the back and unload beyond the archway. John was driving a jeep with a double pony trailer attached, and as soon as he was clear of the drive they could get behind to see Sara's lovely grey face sticking out at the back. She did not look at all worried and was obviously used to travelling.

Mrs Tallis came out then, and told him:

'There's room to turn round at the back.'

It took another two minutes for John to park the trailer, then he and Mrs Tallis unbolted the ramp and let it down. John untied Sara and led her out.

Lissa and Cass stroked her velvety nose and patted her neck. She searched for something to eat and seemed highly offended when they had nothing to offer.

'Where are you going to put her?' John asked.

'We thought we'd put her in the loose-box for a little while until she gets used to us, then turn her out in the field.'

'Have you got something to tempt her with, make her feel at home?'

'I'll get something,' Cass said, and disappeared towards the kitchen.

'Another couple of weeks, and she can stay out all the time without a rug. She's still wearing one at night, though it's getting quite mild,' John explained.

'So she can live out now at night-time?' mother asked.

'Yes, but keep the rug on a bit longer because she's been used to it. In actual fact she's a tough pony and shouldn't need it but our lot are all a bit pampered. Mrs Beech treats them even better than her own children.'

'What is she like to catch?'

'Just puts her nose in the halter, stands there waiting. Well, let's put her in the box and let her have a look round.'

Cass came back then with a bucket which she tried to place in such a way that her mother would not see what was in it. But Mrs Tallis was curious. 'Oh, Cass!' she exclaimed. For in the bucket was a generous mixture of porridge oats, carrots, sliced lengthways, apples and a few slices of brown bread.

John looked in the bucket and roared with laughter. 'She'll cost you a fortune, this one, if that's how you're going to feed her. Now, don't you go giving her any more oats. A pony like this don't need oats. Get her some of them pony-nuts and a bit of barley and bran. That'll do her nicely when you've got her kept in.'

Cass blushed. 'It's a special treat, just this once.'

'I thought she would only want grass in the summer,' said Mrs Tallis.

'So she will,' replied John 'unless you're doing a lot of heavy work, but I don't think you will be. If you're taking her to a show, it's not a bad idea to give her a bit of extra feed or she could get tired and lose condition. It's only when it gets colder, round about September when the grass isn't as good, that you have to think about winter feed. If the weather is *really* bad, and you need to keep her in overnight, she'll need three feeds a day. Have you got some hay in?'

'Not yet. Where do we get it from?' asked Mrs Tallis.

'Mr Crawford has plenty. He'll let you have some reasonable.'

Sara was put in the box and, with her little face looking out over the door, the stable-yard came alive at last.

'I've got all her stuff in the jeep,' said John. He unloaded the tack and the rug, and a nameplate with Sara's name on it.

'Do you think we could ride her?' asked Lissa.

'She's your pony now, you do what you want. Shall I give you a hand?'

'No, thanks. We can manage.' Cass replied.

'Well, I'll be on my way, then. Now, any problem, anything at all, and you give us a call. We'd much rather know, so don't forget.

'We won't,' the girls promised.

As soon as he was gone, they fetched the grooming kit and went over Sara with the dandy brush and the hoof-pick and comb. It did not really need doing, but they wanted to do it.

'Don't brush too much,' Lissa reminded Cass. 'She needs all the grease in her coat for protection.'

'I know!' Cass cried indignantly.

Sara turned round to look at them and smell them curiously as they worked on her. Mrs Tallis stood watching and could not help smiling affectionately at the friendly little pony.

'Can I ride her now?' asked Ginny.

'I suppose so,' Lissa answered, 'but only after us.'

They put the saddle on first and did the girth up loosely to start with, then the bridle. Sara stood with her head lowered and obediently opened her teeth for the bit.

'Isn't she sweet!' cried Cass. 'She's so good, Ginny could saddle her.'

'Can I do it next time then?' Ginny asked.

'We'll teach you,' Lissa replied. 'Come on, now.'

She took the reins and walked across the yard under the archway with Sara following behind her. She heard the lovely sound of hooves clipping the cobblestones, and the world was a wonderful place just then. Sara gave a snort, and the sound echoed round the old brick walls. It did not seem possible that only a few days ago she was saying goodbye to all the ponies at the stables, thinking that was the end of their pony days, and now, out of the blue, they had their own pony to ride, a field to keep her in, and a stable-yard. If only Merlin could be here too.

They reached the field gate with Cass, Mrs Tallis and Ginny close behind. Cass said she wanted to go first this time, so Lissa let her tighten the girth and held the other stirrup leather while Cass mounted. She decided to do a complete tour of the field so that Sara could get to know her new home.

'We need to find somewhere for a schooling ring where we can set up markers,' Lissa told her mother.

'Won't a corner of the field do?' her mother asked.

'Yes, if we can't find anywhere else, but it won't be very good for the grass. It would be better if we could find somewhere else.'

'You do what you like dear, just as long as it's not in my vegetable patch.'

'There is that piece at the side, by the hedge. It's covered with nettles and brambles at the moment, but we could clear it,' Lissa mused.

'It sounds like a big job,' her mother replied.

'Well, we can manage in the field for a while, but it would be nice to have a proper school.'

'Later on I hope to have the whole garden cleared. Everyone keeps saying how nice it used to look. Wouldn't it be lovely to have a garden we could actually go and sit in?'

'We can all help with that, Mummy. It will be fun. I just wish Cass would hurry up, that's all, it's my turn now.'

'You had better let me see your book on horse management. I think I ought to know something about it myself. There seems to be a bit more involved than you two led me to think.'

'I dug it out yesterday. It's under the coffee-table.'

'Can I have a go now?' Ginny asked as Cass approached with Sara.

'No. It's my turn. We'll have to put the stirrups right

65

up for you,' Lissa told her firmly and she scowled a little when she saw how hard Sara was blowing when Cass pulled up.

'You didn't canter her did you?' she asked anxiously.

'No, that's just from trotting. She's terribly out of condition. I should let her have a rest before you get on.'

Sara put her head down and began urgently cropping the grass.

'I'm going to make a start on the supper,' said Mrs Tallis, who was still rather dazed by the day's events, and turning towards the house called over her shoulder, 'Shout for me if you need any help.'

The three girls stood and watched Sara crop the grass until she stopped blowing, then Lissa got up, let the stirrups down one hole, turned some circles in the grass and cut imaginary figures of eight and serpentines at a walk and trot. After about ten minutes she generously said that Ginny could have a ride. They put the leathers up to the highest hole but, as the stirrups were still too long, they twisted the leather round the top of the stirrup once which made them just right. Ginny had her first lesson. Her face was radiant as she clung with one hand to the pommel, and Cass said kindly that she had a natural seat and would soon learn.

It was beginning to get dark, so Cass went to the tack-room for the rug. They took off the saddle, fitted the rug, then slipped off the bridle. Sara dipped away from them in delight and immediately rolled over in the grass, backwards and forwards. When she finally got to her feet, she began the serious business of filling her large stomach, Lissa felt she could have stood there all night, leaning on the gate and watching the pony cropping away contentedly. As the light began to fail, Sara's pale grey coat stood out almost luminously against the shadows. The evening was so quiet and still, just a few sleepy birds twittering, and a cow lowing from the nearby field.

'What a perfect evening.' Cass sighed.

Seven

The next few days passed in a whirl of activity. The cottage was completed, and Lissa now called it The Doll's-house, with its pretty little curtains and papered walls, and all the necessary furniture neatly in place. With the additions of a mirror, a vase and some cushions, everyone agreed that it looked very comfortable.

Every morning about eight o'clock, Cass and Lissa would get up and slip out to the field. They would catch Sara, who stood quietly while one of them slipped on the headcollar, then they would tie her to the gate and give her a light going-over with the brush and finally pick out her feet.

In the corner of the field, next to the stable block, they had marked out a school with an assortment of small boxes lettered in black paint. Here they took it in turns to do some very simple school-work, mainly at a walk. Sara improved every day as she became more used to exercise, just as Mrs Beech had told them she would, and soon a single gentle kick was enough to get a response. She seemed to enjoy working, and her little native ears were always pricked forwards. Every now and then, when she began to get hot, they rested her and after about an hour she would have a few carrots for a reward and would then be turned out again. After that they would go back to the house for breakfast, and begin the tedious task of getting the living-room ready for painting.

After tea, Cass and Lissa would catch Sara again and take her out for a quiet hack along the lane to the heath, where they could ride along the glorious, wide track they had first seen from the car.

Towards the end of the week, they were all so engrossed in work that, at ten one morning when the phone rang, they all wondered who it could be. Mrs Tallis picked up the receiver.

'Who? About the . . . oh, of course! The cottage.' After a short conversation she put down the phone and smiled.

'A possible tenant,' she announced. 'Someone has seen out advertisement.'

'Man or woman?' Cass asked.

'A woman.'

'What did she sound like?'

'Well, it's hard to say. A bit . . . efficient.'

The phone rang again.

'Hello,' said Mrs Tallis. 'About the cottage? Yes, I do have someone coming to see it, but nothing is settled . . .'

After that the phone rang constantly for two or three days and, even after a week, enquiries were still coming in. The girls decided to stay out of the way as much as possible and took Sara out for long hacks up on the hill.

Mrs Tallis found it very hard to decide on a tenant because, although some people found the cottage too small or too out-of-the-way, one or two were quite desperate for somewhere to live, like the young student who came on the second day while Cass and Lissa were painting the living-room. They thought he looked rather nice, but as he had no money, Mrs Tallis thought he might not be able to keep up the payments. It was while he was cycling away that the red car came shooting up the driveway, narrowly missing the bicycle. Cass saw it all from the window, and said:

'He was driving too fast. It was his fault.'

'Who?' asked Lissa

Through the window they saw a man get out of the red car, a thin man, fairly tall, with black, curly hair and dark glasses. He was quite tanned, although it was only April. They saw him look at his watch, take off his glasses, and then he looked directly back at them both with a dark, piercing gaze as they stared at him through the window. Both girls withdrew in confusion.

'Who is that?' Cass hissed.

'He must be the three o'clock one: Mummy already has that couple looking round. He's too early.'

He was already ringing at the doorbell. The girls stared at each other. The bell rang again, impatiently.

'We'd better answer it,' said Lissa. She opened the door cautiously, and said, 'Yes?'

'I phoned about the cottage,' he said, with an edge of sarcasm to his voice. 'Is your mother here?'

'She's over there now, showing someone round. You're not due till three o'clock,' Lissa spoke through the half-open door.

'I know. Where do I go?'

'Through that gateway there. But you're too early.'

'Thank you!' he said, with exaggerated politeness. Lissa thought of the saying 'if looks could kill' and suddenly knew what it meant.

'He looks like someone,' Cass said afterwards, 'I mean, someone who is somebody.'

'Well, I don't like him,' announced Lissa.

'Well, I don't suppose Mummy will like him very much

70

either. Come on, let's go and see Sara.'

On the way to the field, the two girls peered through the archway and saw their mother standing talking to the black-haired man outside the yellow door. They were laughing.

'Oh, I hope she doesn't take him,' Lissa whispered fervently.

Sara lifted her head and made a noise of welcome when the girls approached.

'She likes us!' Cass said.

'I hope she's not lonely,' Lissa replied. 'She is used to having lots of other horses around.'

The last of Sara's heavy coat was falling away, leaving the smooth, milky-white fur of summer, but she still had the whiskery face of a native pony.

'We could trim her whiskers off when we take her to a show,' said Cass. 'People do.'

'I like her the way she is,' Lissa said, rubbing her face against the pony's neck. Sara turned her head to nuzzle her gently and take the red apple that Lissa had stolen from the kitchen.

Soon she was saddled, Lissa mounted, and they walked down the path under the arch and through the hedge, just as the red car drove away. Mrs Tallis stood in the open doorway, a frown on her face.

'Have you decided on anyone?' Lissa called anxiously.

Their mother walked thoughtfully towards them. 'No, I haven't. But Mr Hennessy —'

'Is he the one in the red car?'

'Yes. He wants it quite desperately. He's staying in a hotel at the moment.'

'So are you going to let him move in?' Lissa asked, patting Sara's neck. The pony was, after all, the initial cause of this whole chain of happenings.

'I don't know. I said I must keep these other appointments tomorrow, so I couldn't let him know right away.'

'Well, we're going to take Sara for some exercise. We put all the brushes away,' said Cass.

'Good,' Mrs Tallis said, 'and listen, girls, I think it's time you had a break from all this painting work. You'll be starting school soon . . .'

'School!' they both cried in disgust.

'Yes, school. I was talking to Mrs Crawford yesterday, and the school in Chaseford is not only the nearest, it's the best one for miles around. So tomorrow we'll sort out your school things, and on Monday I'll go down there and see the head.'

'Oh, Mummy, do we have to? Can't you teach us?'

'Of course I can't. If I didn't send you to school, they'd come and arrest me. Besides, you'll make lots of friends there – it will be good for you.'

'I hate school,' Lisa wailed.

'No you don't. And don't tell yourself that before you've given it a chance.'

'It's not fair.' Lissa gave Sara a sudden kick, and the pony woke up in surprise and broke into a trot. 'Sorry,' she whispered, stroking Sara's neck. 'I just wish we didn't have to go to school, and I wish we didn't have to let the cottage.' Lissa felt disturbed. She realised it was not going to be easy having a stranger living amongst them, disrupting the calm of their new-found happiness, and yet it was only because of a total stranger that they were able to have Sara at all. It would not have been possible otherwise.

'Lissa,' Cass said, her hand on Sara's neck as she looked up anxiously into Lissa's face, 'it won't be as bad as the last school. You'll see.' Cass could be very kind sometimes.

'It will,' Lissa said. 'I never can make friends the way you do.'

'It was just bad luck, though. That gang could easily have been in a different class, and then you wouldn't have been picked on.'

'They said I smelled.'

'Well, you shouldn't have gone to muck out Merlin on your way to school.'

'But I didn't want him standing in a dirty box all day.'

Cass grinned. 'It's a nice smell, anyway.'

Reluctantly, Lissa laughed and felt better but she still felt uneasy, as if something awful was going to happen. She supposed it was partly because they were about to be invaded by strangers and lose that magic sense of being shut off from the world.

Suddenly, the bombshell fell.

That evening, while Lissa was peacefully reading a pony book and Cass was drawing a horse going over a jump, the phone rang again. Mrs Tallis picked up the receiver. It was Mrs Beech. Quite suddenly their mother's voice became very quiet and strained. The girls looked up anxiously and watched her face. She glanced at them once, then turned to stare out of the window as she talked.

'Mrs Beech? You have? What is it . . .' There was a long silence, then: 'I see. Yes, it is. Very unfortunate. I'm sorry, too. Of course, we knew it might happen, but not as soon as this. They'll be heart-broken . . . Thank you, but I don't think . . . all right, we'll think about it. Thank you for letting me know. Two days . . . very well. Goodbye.'

Mrs Tallis put down the receiver looking very serious

indeed. The girls stared at her, but she avoided their gaze. Lissa felt numb. She knew something awful was happening. Mrs Beech was going to take Sara away again, it could only be that. She was too shocked even to cry.

'What did she say?' asked Cass.

'She has to sell Sara.'

'Oh! The beast, the beast!' Cass screamed, and she flung herself on the sofa and beat the cushions with her fists.

'Why?' Lissa whispered.

'It seems her daughter has seen a pony she wants very much; one of her friends at school is selling it, and she can't have it unless they sell Sara first. Mrs Beech was very apologetic, but of course we knew it might happen.'

'No. It's not true. How can they be so horrible. I hate her!' Cass wailed between sobs of rage.

Lissa felt sick. 'I think I'll go outside for a while,' she said.

Mrs Tallis went on: 'To be fair, she did say she'd give us first option, she'll give us a couple of days to think about it.'

'Think about what?' Lissa asked.

'Well, if we wanted to buy Sara, she'd let us have her for £450 with tack. Of course, it's out of the question. We can't possibly afford it.'

Both girls stared at her, a tiny seed of hope in their hearts just refusing to be crushed.

'She's given us a couple of days?' Cass asked, suddenly calm again.

'I told you, it's out of the question. It might just as well be four thousand pounds. Don't even think about it.'

74

'There must be some way of raising the money. How much rent money would there be?'

'I suppose I can ask for a month in advance, but that money is for food and shoes and insurance; if we use it up what will we do later? Anyway, the electric wiring needs doing, it's in a dangerous condition. Really, Cass, if you start talking about buying her, I shall get very angry.'

'But if we could raise the money ourselves in some way, or sell something.'

'We could each get a Saturday job,' Lissa put in.

'Don't be silly, you can't find £450 in two days. I mean it, I don't want to hear any more about it. I'm sorry you're disappointed, but that's final.'

A moody silence ensued. Finally, Lissa could bear it no longer, so she left the room and went to see Sara.

In the paddock, Sara stopped eating to turn to look at her. Lissa put her arms round the sturdy neck and pressed her face into the soft grey fur. She could not bring herself to tell Sara the news because her heart would definitely break. After waiting patiently for a while, Sara shook herself free and went on eating.

Eight

'The trouble with you,' Cass said, 'is that you give up so easily. We are going to keep Sara. The only question is how.'

'But Mummy said . . .'

'She always comes round. Don't you know that by now?'

'Not when she's this angry. And we'll never find the money.'

'Yes, we will. Let's go and have a think.'

Together they climbed the gate and made their way to the chestnut trees. In a couple of minutes they were in their favourite perch, the only place where any serious thinking could be done. Lissa pressed her palms into the trunk and whispered: 'Help us tree. I promise to protect all trees forever if you help us now.'

'We could pick daffodils from the garden and sell them up on the lay-by,' Cass suggested. 'There must be thousands of them, and lots of people use that road.'

'At 50p a bunch? In two days?' Lissa replied in despair. 'Isn't there something we could sell? Something really valuable?'

'You mean like the gold brooch you had for your christening? And I've got the bracelet. I bet they're worth quite a lot.'

76

'Mother would never let us sell them!' Lissa cried, shocked.

'No,' Cass agreed.

'If only there was more time, we could wash cars or run errands.'

'Do you think anyone would buy any of my paintings?' asked Cass.

'It's possible, I suppose. Some of them are quite good.'

'If we could persuade Mummy to go into town tomorrow, I could take a few into the gift shop and see what they say.'

'Would you dare?' Lissa asked in admiration.

'To save Sara? You bet I would.'

'Then I'll take some flowers and see if I can sell some. There will be more chance in the town. Only I don't think Mummy would like it very much, so don't tell her till afterwards.'

They both felt better now they were planning some positive action.

At tea, Cass asked casually; 'Were you thinking of going into town tomorrow, Mummy?'

'Why, do you want something? asked her mother.

'I would quite like to go to the gift shop . . . for my painting . . .'

'I do want to go in, as a matter of fact. We're almost out of flour and coffee, and I want to see the electrician.'

Cass and Lissa exchanged triumphant glances.

'It would be nice to look at paper for the living-room, even though we can't get it just yet,' Lissa suggested, needing time to sell her flowers. Her mother began to look suspicious. Cass kicked Lissa's ankle under the table. Lissa simply did not have the knack and she almost blushed.

The moment passed and soon it was bedtime. Cass furtively sorted out a dozen of her best paintings, most of which were of ponies in a landscape setting. Lissa cut out a piece of cardboard and carefully wrote on it in felt-tip: *Daffodils for sale, 50p a bunch.* Then she set the alarm to wake her up very early. That night she slept only for brief spells and in between she lay awake worrying. When the alarm finally rang she had only just begun to sleep soundly and felt unbearably tired.

It was a damp and misty morning. Lissa put on a mac and went out in the gloomy light taking with her a large pair of scissors and a cardboard box. She picked only the flowers that were half open, as they would last longer, and soon had the box full. In the hedge she found some pretty sprays of leaves, and she gathered an armful of those as well. Then in the shelter of the shed she tied them into little bunches of ten blooms with one spray of leaves, which took a long time. When at last she was ready to hide the box in the boot of the car there were sounds of movement coming from the kitchen.

'You're up early,' Mrs Tallis said. Lissa opened her mouth to reply, but her mother had turned her back and was busy preparing breakfast, so she just said, 'What time are we leaving?'

'As soon as we're ready. No point wasting time so don't be long, we'll have breakfast in a minute.'

Lissa brushed her hair well and put on clean jeans and her best sweatshirt. She felt nervous. Cass was already dressed. She had put on her one and only smart pair of trousers, a sweater and black shoes. She had a secretive air about her, slightly defiant too. Lissa wished she could feel as brave as Cass. All the way into town her thoughts were so jumbled and confused that she hardly heard anything her mother said. At one point Mrs Tallis asked:

'What is the matter with you, Lissa? Oh, I suppose it's because of Sara. Really, there will be other ponies. One day, I promise you.'

Fortunately Ginny stayed with her mother on that trip into town and Mrs Tallis assumed that Lissa would accompany Cass to the craft shop, so the parting was easily arranged. As soon as they were out of sight, Lissa crept back to the car to fetch her box of flowers. It was a very large one, filling both her arms, so that she could hardly see where she was going.

'Cass, will you help me find somewhere to sell them?' Lissa said desperately. 'As far from here as possible?'

'Oh, Lissa, I've got my paintings to carry!' Cass said.

'Please.'

So they walked along the High Street until, on the other side of the lights, they found a suitable place in a recess next to a very busy corner. Lissa propped up her sign, put her box on the ground and felt very foolish.

'Pick them up, like they do in the market,' said Cass.

'Fifty pence a bunch,' Lissa said weakly, and Cass almost collapsed in giggles.

'Here, hold these!' she said, handing Lissa her paintings. Taking a bunch in each hand Cass boldly accosted an old woman with a shopping bag:

'Fifty pence a bunch. We picked them this morning.'

'I've got plenty in my own garden,' replied the woman, and walked on. Behind her, however, was a young woman pushing a pram and she stopped to look. 'That's cheap,' she said, 'I'll have two.' Cass and Lissa grinned at each other.

'Two bunches for a pound!' yelled Cass, attracting the

attention of more passers-by. Lissa propped the paintings against the wall and joined in.

'Is this for charity?' someone asked.

'Yes, it's for Save a Pony.' replied Cass.

'You shouldn't have said that,' Lissa said afterwards.

'It's true, isn't it?' said Cass. 'Look, you can manage now, so I'll go along to the craft shop.'

Lissa found she was quite enjoying herself. People were so kind. 'All right, I'll see you later,' she said. 'Don't be long.'

Cass picked up her paintings and hurried away. Lissa saw her enter the craft shop on the other side, then she was busy for a while so she could not see whether Cass came out again or not.

About half the flowers were now sold. Lissa, feeling very tired, dreaded seeing her mother come looking for her. It was nearly half past eleven, and there was still no sign of Cass.

There were so many people on the street that someone nearly kicked her box over by mistake, and Lissa climbed up on a nearby bench.

'Fifty pence a bunch, two for a pound,' she shouted.

'I'll take four,' a lady said, 'Is it for charity?'

'It's to save our pony,' Lissa replied. She was getting worried. Where was Cass? Was their mother waiting at the car, by now really angry? What would she say?

Eventually Cass reappeared, but from another direction. She looked different, and rather subdued.

'How did you get on?' Lissa asked anxiously.

Cass shrugged. 'They don't buy paintings outright. They put them in the window and if they sell you get two-thirds of the price and the shop keeps the rest.'

'That's not fair, you did all the work.'

'It's to cover overheads, she said, whatever they are. Anyway, she kept the two best ones but she didn't want any of the others. If any get sold, she's going to phone me.'

Lissa climbed down off the bench. 'So it's no good then? You won't get the money in time and all I've got is a measly eight pounds.'

Cass muttered something else which Lissa could not hear.

'What did you say?'

'I've sold the christening presents,' Cass said.

She looked at Lissa with eyes full of fear. 'Well, I had to do something.'

Lissa gasped.

'Mummy will be furious. You should have asked her first.'

'She'd have said no. She doesn't care if we keep Sara or not.' Cass looked at the ground in misery.

'How much did you get?'

'Thirty-five pounds for my brooch, and I got fifty for your bracelet.'

'It's still not enough.'

The two girls looked at each other in despair.

'We'd better go and find Mummy,' said Lissa at last.

'What's she going to say to us?' asked Cass, her voice shaking.

Lissa picked up her box and together they made their way back to the car park. Mrs Tallis was sitting waiting impatiently in the car. 'Wherever have you been? We've been waiting for ages,' she said.

'Better get it over with,' Lissa whispered.

'What have you got there?' her mother demanded, looking at the box. Lissa knew from her tone that she was building up to a row.

'I've done an awful thing,' Cass announced. 'You're going to be terribly angry.'

Her mother looked at her with raised eyebrows, waiting for her to go on. Putting the cardboard box in the boot, Lissa thought: It's not what people do that makes others angry, it's the frame of mind that leads them to do it. Cass thought the end result was all that mattered and Mummy would get over her rage in time. But that's not the point. It's as if people are joined together by a mass of tiny strands and each time you hurt someone, one of the strands is broken.

Cass had, by now, told her mother the whole story and Mrs Tallis was staring back at Cass in amazement.

'I see,' Mrs Tallis said, and was quiet for a moment. 'Where is the money?'

'Here,' Cass replied, taking out her purse.

'I think you'll find they were worth rather more than that. Go back to the shop and tell the man you want them back.' She said it quite calmly, but in the sort of voice that no one would dream of disobeying.

'Lissa didn't know anything about it,' Cass said, then turned and walked slowly back up the road. Lissa hesitated, then ran after her and took her hand.

'I hate her,' said Cass.

'Don't be silly,' Lissa replied.

The man in the shop was annoyed at Cass for wasting his time, but he returned the brooch and the bracelet, and took back his money.

No one spoke all the way back in the car.

In the afternoon the phone rang. It was Mrs Beech wanting to know if they had come to a decision about whether or not they wanted to buy Sara. Someone else was very interested in her and wanted to come and look her over, so could she send John with the trailer tomorrow morning to pick her up? Mrs Tallis said that she could.

So that was it. The end of the dream.

Lissa and Cass spent the rest of that awful day grooming Sara and polishing her hooves, and cleaning the tack to perfection.

Then they sat up in the tree, watching her until it was dark.

Soon after eleven the next morning, John arrived and took Sara away. He didn't say very much, but a glance at their faces told him everything, and he gave them both a kindly pat on the shoulder before he drove off.

It was a black day. Cass stayed up in the tree and

refused to come down for lunch. If anything, she was even more upset than Lissa because she loved Sara to distraction, but at the back of Lissa's mind was a vague doubt. It was money they didn't have and couldn't afford to spend, but on top of that, if they were going to buy a pony after all, she would rather it was Merlin. Merlin, who was a long way away, who would never even be for sale, and if he was, would cost twice as much as Sara. But these were thoughts that never even came to the suface of her mind to be defined; she simply felt confused.

When at last Cass came in, she went up to her room and stayed there. Lissa went to see her once, but Cass was crying and wouldn't let her in.

The next day the phone rang again. It was Mr Hennessy, the man in the red car. Mrs Tallis was talking to him for nearly half an hour. The girls could hear snatches of conversation:

'No, I haven't decided yet . . . yes, it would help, of course, but I'm not at all sure . . . Let me think about it. Yes, I have . . .' Then a very long pause while Mr Hennessy seemed to do all the talking.

When Mrs Tallis came off the phone she looked rather bewildered. 'I hope I've done the right thing,' she said.

'What have you done?' asked Lissa. Cass had decided not to speak unless spoken to.

'I've told Mr Hennessy he can have the cottage.'

'Oh, Mummy!' Lissa cried, looking at her mother in horror. Without any Sara for compensation, it seemed an unnecessary hardship to have Mr Hennessy living so close.

'Why do we have to let it at all?' Cass asked, sulkily. 'After all, the money isn't so desperate now.'

Mrs Tallis looked at them both for several moments,

then reluctantly explained, 'He offered three months' rent in advance.'

They both stared back at their mother, wide-eyed, as this piece of news took some time to sink in. Also, it was hard to read her expression; whether it made any difference to the situation, or whether she was already planning other things.

'Does that mean . . .' Cass finally asked, not daring to go on. Lissa held her breath. Mrs Tallis frowned sternly at them both, then sighed; she was unsuccessfully trying to stop a wide grin from spreading over her face. 'We can?' Cass yelled, then flew at her mother's neck and hugged and kissed her. Lissa behind her was fighting for a gap.

'Oh, Mummy darling.'

'Less of the Mummy darling, and a bit more common sense. I might be able to get some of the wiring done now, as well.'

'And by the time we need winter feed and straw and everything, there will be some more rent due,' Cass cried joyfully.

'I think I'm being awfully foolish,' said Mrs Tallis. 'In fact, I'm beginning to think this pony madness is highly contagious.'

'It is, it is,' Cass shrieked. 'Oh! Oh! It's wonderful.'

'Hurry up and ring Mrs Beech,' Lissa urged, 'because someone else was coming to see Sara.'

'Just give me a moment to collect my wits,' said Mrs Tallis, 'though quite frankly, I think I must have lost them altogether. It must have happened the day we moved in here.' In a moment, she picked up the receiver and dialled Mrs Beech's number.

They were too late. Mrs Beech was very apologetic,

but Sara had already gone. A lady had come to see her the evening before, and had already collected her in a horse-box.

Nine

Mr Hennessy was moving in. The red car was seen to go up and down the drive several times over the course of the day carrying its burden right across the yard, up to the yellow door. Suitcases, boxes, files, equipment of some sort, enormous black cases with wires attached. The girls wondered where he would find the space for everything.

'Now, you keep out of his way,' Mrs Tallis warned. 'I'm sure he's here because he wants privacy.'

Mr Hennessy paid his rent in cash, which Mrs Tallis found rather odd.

'He's a spy,' whispered Lissa. 'He's collecting secret information and transmitting it to the Russians.'

'He doesn't have an aerial,' replied Cass scornfully.

The next morning a white van arrived, carrying folding ladders, and the driver proceeded to climb up on to the cottage roof to fix up an aerial.

'It's a TV aerial,' said Cass.

'It may *look* like a television aerial . . .' Lissa replied significantly.

There were all sorts of jobs to do in the stable-yard, like sweeping up the feed-room, and whilst they were doing them it was fun to invent all kinds of reasons why Mr Hennessy should be hiding away in their cottage. It was all a game.

It stopped being a game on the second evening when Mr Hennessy had a visitor. Lissa was sitting alone, curled up in the straw in the tack-room, when she heard footsteps on the cobblestones. She thought nothing of it until they stopped right under the archway and she heard Mr Hennessy continuing his conversation with his visitor:

'No one must know where I am, Brian – no one.'

'What if I need to get in touch with you? Can I phone the house?'

'I'd rather not. There's a tame landlord down at the Half Moon in Chaseford. He'll take messages for me.'

'You can trust him?'

'He used to be in the business himself.'

'Well, good luck. If this one turns out all right, there'll be contracts coming in from all sides.'

'I can do it so long as they leave me alone. All I need is time.'

'Are you sure you'll be all right?'

'I will now. Thanks for all your help, Brian. If you hadn't got me out of there, I would have gone mad.'

'What if they come looking for you?'

'I've changed my name. You're the only one who knows who I am.'

'Well, if you need anything, call me.'

They moved on then, and the voices faded away. Lissa heard a car start up and drive away, and Mr Hennessy's footsteps as he returned to the cottage.

Lissa sat rigid with fear, stunned by what she had heard. For a long time she was afraid to move in case Mr Hennessy saw her hiding-place and suspected her of listening. It was getting dark when she finally crept out and went to find her mother. She repeated the conversation, word for word as far as she could remember it, and asked her mother what they should do.

Mrs Tallis was kneeling on the floor in the upstairs bedroom, sorting through all their school clothes. She sat back on her heels and looked thoughtfully at Lissa.

'I don't think we should jump to conclusions, Lissa, although it does sound very fishy.'

'But it sounds as though he's escaped from somewhere. Why else should he change his name?'

'There may be all kinds of reasons. If he's escaped from prison we should have read something about it in the paper, and there would be a description. Try not to worry. I'll keep an eye on him. Just make sure you girls stay out of his way.'

Lissa felt that her mother was taking it too lightly, but she was relieved that someone else was in charge of the situation. However, that night she was unable to sleep and after she heard her mother go to bed around midnight, Lissa found herself creeping down the stairs to check that all the doors were locked and bolted, and that all the windows were closed. It was the first time in her life that she had ever done such a thing. Three nights in a row this happened, and then Mrs Tallis came down the stairs and demanded to know what she was doing.

'I just wanted to make sure the house was locked,' Lissa explained.

'Darling, I always lock the house, and I check everything twice, you can trust me. No wonder you look so tired lately. Now, please, go to sleep.'

For three or four days after that they saw nothing of Mr Hennessy. In the morning the curtains of the cottage were drawn till midday. He never went out until evening, around nine, and they never heard him come back, except once when Lissa woke to the sound of the car and noticed the sky was getting light. Once Lissa saw him across the yard as he carried some rubbish to the dustbin and he waved in quite a cheery way. Perhaps he was perfectly normal after all and there was nothing to worry about.

After a while she stopped worrying about him altogether, because the dreaded day loomed when they had to start school, and this monstrous thought squeezed all other fears from her head.

'Well, how did you get on?' Mrs Tallis asked on their first day, as Cass and Lissa detached themselves from the crowd outside the school gates and climbed into the car. Ginny was already sitting in the back as the first school finished twenty minutes earlier.

'All right,' Lissa muttered, staring out of the car window at the mass of humanity, shouting, kicking, and swinging school-bags.

'There's Angie!' Cass cried, opening the window. 'Angie!' she shrieked.

'Please,' Mrs Tallis said, covering her ears.

A small child with one dark-brown pigtail falling down her back was getting into a large yellow car. She turned to wave at Cass.

'She's in my class. She's got her own pony and her father drives her to shows in a horse-box. She's really nice.'

'You're lucky. I've got a horrible monster called Teresa sitting behind me. She got me into trouble. She kept pulling my hair until I yelled, and Miss Fox sent us both out of the room. On the first day!'

'Can't you sit somewhere else?' her mother suggested.

'There isn't anywhere. Then in French, Mandy Morris – she sits next to Teresa – kept digging me in the back with a pencil. I *hate* school,' Lissa said with feeling.

It was a relief to turn into the wilderness of White Trees Farm and leave the outside world behind. The driveway, which their mother had cut back a couple of weeks before, was fast becoming overgrown again. The warmth and rain of April had encouraged the long, spiky vines to claim back their territory.

'I ought to dig them out altogether,' Mrs Tallis said, 'but it's an enormous job. I'll just have to cut them back again for now.'

The outside of the house had little to show for all their hard work. It looked much as it did on the first day they saw it, apart from the mended window-panes. Once inside the front door, however, the hall was bright and sunny and lined with books, and the large living-room a pleasure to sit in, with soft beige and white colours, a log fire burning in the evenings, the large familiar chesterfield, an ancient pair of tatty chintz armchairs, and all the comforting oddments from their old home combining to make the room secure and welcoming.

Lissa flung her schoolbag into a corner, slumped into an armchair and threw her school shoes into some hole from which it would take half an hour to recover them in the morning.

'If I leave school at sixteen,' she said, 'I've only got five years to go. Only!'

'You won't leave school at sixteen,' replied her mother.

'I will. I loathe school.'

'What will you do at sixteen?'

'Run a livery stables. Here.'

'I see,' said her mother, laughing. 'Well, you've got lots of time to think about it. I've made a nice coconut cake, so cheer up.' She fetched a tray from the kitchen all ready laid with tea-things.

'I think it's a lovely idea,' Cass said, 'because if I do go to art college, I can help you in the evenings and at weekends.'

'Apart from this girl Teresa, how was the school-work?' Mrs Tallis asked.

'Easy,' said Cass. 'We've got to do a maths test next week to be graded, but it's all things we did last term.'

'I feel like making something,' Lissa said. 'A model or something. What are you doing, Cass?'

'I think I'll do my homework first,' Cass replied.

Lissa finished her tea and hesitated.

'Leave the cups,' said Mrs Tallis. Lissa gave her a grateful hug and was about to run up the stairs when a car pulled up in front of the house. The brakes were slammed on so hard, she could hear the wheels skidding on the gravel. A door slammed loudly, then the outline of a man could be seen through the glass panels of the front door. The doorbell sounded long and hard. Lissa opened the door.

Mr Hennessy stood there, tall and menacing. Behind him she could see the red car in the middle of the driveway. Lissa stared at him in confusion and he stared back with his usual expression of anger and impatience. There was an aura around him so powerful she felt she could reach out her hand and touch it, an air of tense and explosive rage. Instinctively, she stepped back.

'Is your mother here?' It was his first visit to the house since the day he came to look at the cottage.

Mrs Tallis came into the hall. 'Oh, Mr Hennessy!' she said.

Now he appeared to be confused.

'Won't you come in?'

'No . . . I don't like complaining, but . . .'

'Oh dear, have the girls done something?' asked Mrs Tallis.

'No; it's my car. I've just got an almighty scratch down the side from those brambles in the drive. I really think you should have something done about it.'

'I'm so sorry. Where is it?' Mrs Tallis walked past him to the car and looked ruefully at the damage. 'Oh dear, I am sorry. What do you want me to do about it?'

'Don't worry about the car, my garage can fix that up. But please sort out the driveway.'

'I was planning to, but it's grown so quickly.'

'Well, I'll leave it with you.' He was backing away.

'Are you sure you won't come in? Would you like some tea?'

He shuddered visibly: 'No, thank you . . . No time.'

He got in the car and drove round to park in his usual place next to the woodpile.

'What a cheek!' cried Cass. 'He doesn't think our house is good enough to come in.'

'Oh, I don't think that's the reason. He said he hasn't time,' said Mrs Tallis cheerfully.

'I'm glad he didn't come in,' said Lissa forcefully. 'I don't want him contaminating our lovely new home with his beastly moods like he did the stables.'

'Well, I don't think he looks well,' replied Mrs Tallis. 'Did you see how his hands were shaking? I wonder what he meant by no time. What does he do all day?'

'It was just an excuse. I'm glad his car got scratched.'

'Don't be silly. He might move out and demand his money back. Or decide not to stay on when the three months is up.'

'I hope he does. We could find someone else,' said Cass.

'It's not that easy, that much we do know. He's no trouble really, just as long as you keep out of his way. I think I'd better make a start on the drive this evening,' said Mrs Tallis.

'I'll help you,' said Lissa.

It was late afternoon on a fine April day and the garden was still full of daffodils. It was pleasant to work outside, breathing the sweet cool air and creating a green wall from the chaos of vegetation. Two or three hours passed almost unnoticed while they worked. Sometime later Mr Hennessy drove out again, and they stood aside to let him pass.

'That poor man. I wonder if he's lonely,' said Mrs Tallis.

'How can you say that, when he's so horrible?' Lissa asked.

'He's not horrible. You can hardly blame him for being annoyed if his lovely car is scratched.'

'He doesn't have to be so angry.'

'I'm sure he's not well. Either that or he's got a Secret Sorrow.'

'Well,' Lissa said, 'I think he's sinister.'

'Gracious, look at the time!' Mrs Tallis exclaimed. 'It's Ginny's bedtime and we haven't had supper yet. Can you get the wheelbarrow and we'll carry all these cuttings to the dump.'

'I haven't done my homework,' Lissa remembered.

'Oh, Lissa! Well, you'd better do that while I get the supper.'

Together they cleared away the cuttings, then Lissa settled down in the sitting-room with her books.

The log fire was still glowing in the grate, making a lovely flickering light on the walls. Lissa ate her supper while she worked. It was maths, which she found reasonably easy. When it was finished, she looked up to find her mother looking at her thoughtfully.

'What is it?' Lissa asked. She went to sit on the arm of her mother's chair with her arms around her neck.

'Oh I was just thinking about you and Cassandra, how different you are. These children at school that pester you; Cass never seems to have those problems.'

'I know. It's not fair,' Lissa replied.

'I think it must have something to do with your attitude. You seem more vulnerable, somehow, and people always attack someone who looks vulnerable. It's as if you draw them towards you, like a pattern that follows you wherever you go. It happened at your last school, remember? Somehow you have to find a way to change the pattern.'

'I wish I could,' said Lissa fervently.

'When you can see the same thing happening again and again, that's what your father used to call karma. It's something deep in your own life. When you look around you, what you see is a reflection of your life. So, if people are difficult, it's something in you that has to be changed,' her mother said. 'Imagine looking in a mirror to comb your hair, and trying to comb the mirror instead.'

'But how can I stop other people behaving the way they do?'

'I can't tell you what to say. It's what you are that counts, so that you say and do the right thing quite naturally. But you can influence other people much more than you think. Try not to dislike people, treat them with respect even if they behave badly, because most people are nice inside. Once you get your attitude right, the situation often goes away all on its own. You need to tackle this thing now, because to spend the rest of your life being afraid of people is a terrible handicap.'

'What about people who break trees, or beat horses?'

'They are making a bad cause, creating bad karma for themselves. It really is a great privilege to be born a human being and a huge responsibility. Some people don't appreciate it.'

Lissa clung to her mother, watching the fire die down, and nothing seemed to matter quite so much anymore.

Cass was asleep when Lissa finally went to bed. They were now sharing the back bedroom as the damp patch was almost dried out in the fine weather. Tonight the bathroom was freezing when she went for her bath, and the old pipes played their routine game with much thumping and banging. It always made Lissa think of drum majorettes. She felt calm, though, and in the morning, getting ready for school, it seemed as if a week had already passed since the day before. She thought how lucky Cass was to have someone like Angie and wondered if there was anyone in her own class who might turn out to be a friend.

When they arrived at school, Cass said goodbye and dashed away to the playground as soon as the car came to a halt. Lissa hung back. She stood alongside her mother's window and looked into her eyes. Her mother waited for a moment, looked back at her, and then she understood. It was the gesture Lissa used to make each morning at the first school, when she needed courage to go and face the day. It took a few moments to get the right look, the right sense of absolute closeness, then she could break the spell and go. It was like the feeling with the ancient chestnut tree, like drawing strength from life

itself. Finally, Lissa gathered up her satchel and turned
to go in.

At the end of school, Mrs Tallis was late. Cass and
Lissa sat on the wall, waiting. When at last she arrived
she said 'Sorry!' but, rather contradictorily, she didn't
look sorry at all, in fact she had a big smile on her face.

'What's up?' asked Cass, rather indignantly.

'How did you get on?' Mrs Tallis asked Lissa, ignoring
Cass's question.

'How do you mean?' asked Lissa. 'Oh!' She suddenly
remembered; 'You mean Teresa and Mandy? Well, the
first thing this morning Miss Fox came in and said she
was moving them to the front to make them concentrate.
I don't think she likes them very much. I haven't seen
them all day.'

'See what happens when you stop worrying?' her
mother said smugly.

'Something *is* up,' Cass said suspiciously. 'You're hiding something. What is it?'

'I'll tell you when we get home,' said Mrs Tallis, and
no matter how much they tried, they couldn't get her to
say another word.

'It's something to do with the house,' said Lissa.

No reply.

'Mr Hennessy has left?'

Still nothing.

When at last they reached home, Cass said, 'Well?'

'Go and change your clothes, then I'll tell you.'

'That's not fair,' Cass complained, but they did as they
were told, and then Mrs Tallis said:

'I've got something to show you,' and led the way out
of the back door and down to the field. Lissa felt her
heart beating rather fast, and a sudden faint hope entered

her head which she pushed aside. They passed the kitchen garden where the lettuces were now beginning to push through the soil. It couldn't be that! At the paddock gate Mrs Tallis stopped and turned to face them.

It was true. Sara was back. She was happily cropping the grass and lifted her head to give a whicker of welcome, then went on grazing. The girls stared at her in delight and astonishment, then scrambled over the gate to smother her with hugs and caresses.

'But how did it happen?' Cass cried. 'I thought she was sold. How on earth did we get her back?'

'Mrs Beech phoned me this morning,' Mrs Tallis replied. 'She said the other lady had sent Sara back again and were we still interested. There is a snag though. Apparently the other people had a vet to check her over and Sara's got spavin. I suppose you know what that is because I don't. Mrs Beech says it's not all that serious, and it won't make her lame any more, although there could be some stiffness occasionally.'

'Spavin! Where?' Cass cried, while Lissa anxiously asked:

'Are you sure it's not serious?'

'Is it our fault?' Cass asked in a shaky voice, while she searched with her fingers for the evidence.

'No, no, no, Mrs Beech said it's nothing to do with us, Sara has had it for some time and it's really nothing to worry about. It's the off-hind leg. Mrs Beech did try and explain it to me and, from what I can gather, it's a sort of arthritis of the bone.'

'Are you sure she's going to be all right?' the girls kept saying, as they felt the leg in turn.

'Quite sure. Actually, Mrs Beech said if we have any trouble we can send her back.'

98

'Send her back!' said Cass in absolute horror. 'We'll never do that.'

'But is she ours now, or is she still on loan?' Lissa wanted to know.

'Bought and paid for,' Mrs Tallis said, 'so you don't have to worry any more.'

There was only one thing to be done then, and that was to get Sara groomed and tacked up as quickly as possible so they could take her out on the heath. Sara herself seemed to be delighted to be back, and not even the sight of Mr Hennessy crossing the yard from his car could spoil the joy of the evening.

Ten

On Saturday morning, Lissa and Cass were cleaning tack in the tack-room. They had the portable radio on because they were hoping to hear a new song that had just come out. Cass was doing the bridle and Lissa the saddle. They had decided to do it properly and undo all the buckles, wiping over each piece of leather to remove the grease, then soaping it and washing and cleaning all the metal parts with metal polish; bit, stirrup irons, even the buckles. Cass had just started rinsing the bit again to get rid of the taste of polish, when suddenly the yellow door burst open, and Mr Hennessy appeared in the doorway of the tack-room, his eyes wild, his hair literally standing on end.

'Will you stop that bloody row!' he shouted. 'I can't hear myself think.'

And as both girls stared at him, too stunned to move, he strode over to the radio and jabbed at the off-button with one finger, gave them a final glare, and stormed out.

Cass stood as if turned to stone, her hands still in mid-air with the water from the sponge beginning to run down her arm into her sleeve.

After a long silence, Lissa cried: 'Well, what a cheek! It's our yard.'

'I hate him,' Cass announced.

'Mother said you're not to hate people, because you only hurt yourself,' replied Lissa. Then added: 'So do I.'

'Actually, I enjoy hating him. It's a good feeling,' Cass went on, her eyes narrowing with venom as she spoke. 'He's spoilt everything. The stables won't be the same, ever. This was my very favourite place, and now every time I come here I shall think of him sitting up there, listening.'

'Let's tell Mummy,' said Lissa.

They finished putting the tack together, picked up the silent radio and made their way back to the house.

Mrs Tallis was in the kitchen, attempting to make pastry on a small Formica-topped table. She listened to their story with concern.

'Now, I told you to keep away. How could you play a radio right underneath him like that!'

'But, Mummy, it's our yard.'

'It's his cottage. He's paying for it. Now, let's see how loud it was.' With a floury hand she switched the radio on again and the sound filled the kitchen. 'You see,' she said, 'it is too loud. You could have had it on quietly and I expect he wouldn't have said anything.'

'That's not loud,' cried Cass. 'It's only half-on.'

'It's too loud,' her mother said firmly. 'I think adults must have more sensitive ears. Anyway, be on the safe side and don't play in the yard any more. You don't have to.'

'Well, I think he's horrible. I hate him,' Cass said.

'I've told you before, hatred only makes you unhappy, and it won't affect Mr Hennessy in the least.' True enough, they both felt very depressed for the rest of the day, even when Mrs Tallis said they could go out for a picnic ride in the afternoon.

While they caught Sara and got her ready their mother packed a tea for them both with chocolate-spread sandwiches, cheeses covered in foil and apple pies.

Cass rode to start with while Lissa walked, carrying the picnic. Ginny wanted to go with them, but they said she would get tired. Mrs Tallis agreed and offered to teach her how to make a cake instead.

Up on the hills there was a strong wind blowing. The heather stretched for miles around with a criss-cross of small tracks going in all directions, but they stuck to the main gallops which passed close to the brow of the next hill where a group of oak trees stood. They decided to stop there for the picnic, so they loosened Sara's girth, put on the headcollar and let her graze for a while.

Slate-coloured clouds raced across the sky, leaving patches of brilliant blue, and the heath was alternately bright and gloomy as the sun was hidden, then set free. There were hundreds of rabbits and they also saw the tracks of small-hooved animals, probably deer, though they stayed well hidden.

'Where shall we go now?' asked Cass, gathering up the wrapping-papers.

'There's a lake somewhere further on, I saw it from the car. Shall we see if we can find it?' suggested Lissa.

'Yes, let's, I bet Sara could do with a drink.'

The wind was blowing quite strongly now and the trees were making weird noises and bending over at very strange angles. They tightened Sara's girth, put the bit back in her mouth and removed the headcollar. Lissa got up and they took the path back on to the gallops.

There were three horses in the distance coming up behind them along the same track. They were moving quite fast and the girls watched with interest, wondering where they came from. There was plenty of room to pass, and Lissa kept Sara well to the side as they heard the thunder of hooves on turf close behind them.

Sara pricked up her ears and began to fidget. Lissa shortened her reins and patted the pony's neck. 'It's all right. They're going past us. Keep calm,' she said soothingly.

The wind was almost gale force now. It lifted Sara's mane and turned her tail into a streamer, like the end of a kite. She squealed out with excitement. The three horses thundered past and it looked as if the lead horse was

barely under control, its rider leaning back on the reins, pulling violently, shouting: 'Whoa. Steady on.'

Sara squealed again, a long, high-pitched, eerie sound, then suddenly gave one outrageous buck and plunged forward. Lissa was thrown forward on to her neck where she clung, then slipped sideways, her face suspended for several moments beside a flailing hoof. Completely rooted to the spot with terror, Cass watched as her sister hit the ground, as if in slow motion. Lissa's foot caught in the stirrups and for a few strides she was jolted over the rough turf, bouncing like a doll. Cass didn't even realise that she was screaming, her voice carried away on the wind. Then the leather slipped back, out of the well-oiled T-bar, and Sara was free. Lissa lay in a heap on the grass.

'Lissa! Lissa!' Cass wailed in despair. Lissa opened her eyes and stared back at her without moving. Then, very slowly, she eased herself into a sitting position.

'Thank goodness Mrs Beech keeps her tack in good condition,' Cass said with relief. 'It probably saved your life.'

Clinging on to Cass, Lissa got to her feet and very painfully put her weight on each leg in turn to see if it would support her, but her ribs hurt too much to stand upright. She felt numb all over although apart from a lot of bruises, there did not seem to be any injuries, and no bones broken.

'I'll go and catch Sara. You sit here,' Cass said.

Far away on the next hill they could see three dots moving upwards at a fast pace, and some way behind them a white one, showing no sign of flagging.

'No, Cass, let's stick together,' said Lissa. 'It looks as though we've got a long way to go.'

'It's their fault, they ought to catch Sara and bring her back,' Cass said indignantly.

'They probably haven't even seen her. Come on, we'd better not waste any time.'

Lissa's face was white and there was a jagged cut in the velvet of her hat where it had hit a stone. She felt a pang of disappointment for its spoilt beauty but then realised that it might well have been her own head.

They did not talk about the accident because they did not want to think about how close Lissa had been to serious injury. If the stirrup had not come away she could have been dragged for miles.

'Don't tell Mummy,' Lissa said. 'She'll only worry. Just say I fell off and Sara ran away, which she did.'

'If you're all right. You might have to see a doctor,' Cass said, trying not to sound as worried as she felt. She glanced quickly at Lissa's white face and felt sick. Lissa did not reply; she was beginning to ache all over, every muscle feeling as though it had been torn from its moorings. They walked on in silence. Although the horses were now completely out of sight, they still expected at any moment to see Sara grazing at the side of the track, looking sheepish and sorry.

There was no sign of her.

It was a long walk up the next hill. Lissa complained once that her head was hurting and she felt dizzy. The sun was low in the sky and the shadows beginning to lengthen, and as daylight began to fade the girls became more and more anxious.

Now the girls were in the grip of an icy fear. Suppose they could not find Sara. Suppose they never found her. Suppose she had been kidnapped and taken away in a lorry, heading for the meat markets. These things happen.

Suppose she ran across the main road and got hit by a car in the dusky light. She might be dead now, this moment! Cass began to cry silently; salty tears ran down into her mouth. Lissa was too tired to cry. This was the worst kind of nightmare, the kind that went on and on with no ending.

Finally, they came to a road with a steady succession of cars passing by. The traffic was not too fast, a pony could be lucky and pass through it. If only they knew which way to go.

They decided to turn right, because it seemed logical that the leading horses would circle back the way they had come and Sara would follow them. It was a lonely road with no houses for about a mile, but at last they came to a small bungalow set back from the road.

'We'd better ask if we can phone Mummy,' Cass said. 'She'll be worried.' Lissa remained silent, as though sleep-walking, so Cass knocked on the door, which was opened no more than a couple of centimetres. Cass asked if she might use a telephone and the voice of an elderly woman said, 'You go away,' and the door was shut. Cass stood there, not knowing what to do. She turned and glanced at Lissa's white face. The next house might be another mile along the road, and she didn't think Lissa could make it.

She knocked again. This time the letter-box moved.

'I know you kids these days, trying to grab an old woman's pension. Well, you're not coming in my house. Go away.'

'Oh, please,' Cass cried, 'if you won't let us in, can you please phone my mother. Lissa's had an accident.'

After a long pause the door opened again slightly and a woman with white hair peered past Cass to where Lissa stood, looking as if she was about to fall down. The porch light came on, making them both blink. 'You'd better come in then,' she said grudgingly. 'The phone's over there.'

Grateful for the lack of questions, Cass dialled the operator and asked to reverse the charge. Presently her mother's anxious voice was on the line. All Cass's good intentions flew out of the window at the reassuring sound of her mother's voice and she immediately burst into sobs. At first she could not make herself understood, but eventually managed to squeeze out the words: 'We've lost Sara.'

'Where are you? What's happened?'

The woman who owned the cottage firmly took the receiver out of her hands.

'Hello. Are you their mother? There are two girls here and they seem to have lost their pony . . . One of them looks a bit shaken up . . . I'm at the Lodge near the Foxholes car park . . . About twenty minutes? Mrs Bartram is my name.'

After that she was really quite kind. Lissa was made to sit in a chair while Mrs Bartram went to make them a cup of tea, saying she was sorry to be suspicious but you can't be too careful these days, you see such awful stories in the paper, and they could have been pretending. After the cup of tea, some colour came back into Lissa's face. Soon they heard a car pull up and Mrs Bartram went to open the door.

'Are you all right?' Mrs Tallis asked immediately.

'Lissa fell off,' explained Cass. 'Some horses went by too fast and Sara got excited.'

'I'm only a bit bruised. But what are we going to do about Sara? We've looked everywhere,' Lissa wailed.

'I'm taking you home first, then I'll do some phoning round to see if anyone has seen her. Maybe she's gone back to Mrs Beech's place.' While she talked, Mrs Tallis was feeling Lissa all over to check for damage.

'Suppose she gets hit by a car,' Cass said.

'I should think she's grazing quietly somewhere, so try not to worry too much.'

Mrs Tallis thanked Mrs Bartram for all her help, and Mrs Bartram said it was a pleasure to have visitors, and at long last they got into the car.

The first thing Mrs Tallis did when they got home was to call the police in case there had been any accidents involving a pony, but no, much to everyone's relief there had not. Then she looked up all the local riding schools in the phone book to see if Sara had followed the three horses home. This also drew a blank. The list of farms in the phone book was endless; they rang about six of the nearest and then, very reluctantly, Mrs Tallis rang Mrs Beech, who was understandably very worried, and who had no news either.

Then, at about nine-thirty a sergeant from the police station rang. They had just received a call from a Mr Bleckman who owned a poultry farm on the edge of a village. He had gone to check his hens that evening and found a strange white pony grazing on his front verge. He had caught it and put it in his field for the night and called the police. The sergeant gave Mrs Tallis the phone number and she called Mr Bleckman right away.

'I'll go over right away and make sure it's Sara,' Mrs Tallis said.

'I'll come with you,' said Cass.

'I really think you should go to bed,' said her mother.

'I shan't sleep at all unless I know for sure that she's all right,' said Cass frantically.

'Oh, all right. But Lissa at least should go to bed,' she said, 'and in the morning I'll call the doctor.' Lissa did not argue. She did not feel very well and was glad to get into bed and go to sleep. Ginny was already asleep, so Mrs Tallis locked up the house and she and Cass set off together.

Following the map, they found the village and the smallholding and went to knock on the door. Mr Bleckman was surprisingly friendly, considering the time of night. In fact, he seemed to regard it all as a bit of a joke. He showed them the field where he had put the pony.

'Sara!' Cass cried at once. 'You naughty pony!' In the moonlight her unmistakable grey coat glowed, making her look like a ghost horse. Sara whinnied and butted Cass affectionately, hoping to go home. Cass dug some mints out of her pocket and gave them to her.

'We'll have to leave her till tomorrow, if that's all right,' said Mrs Tallis. 'We don't have a pony trailer.'

'That's all right, she'll be fine in here. Not even a chicken could get through that hedge,' said Mr Bleckman.

'We'll see you in the morning then. And thank you very much.'

When they got back, although it was almost eleven o'clock, they rang Mrs Beech to tell her the good news and she offered to send John with the trailer to get Sara home. Mrs Tallis was very grateful for the offer, although Cass said it made them look very feeble, as if they were incapable of riding their own pony back over the heath.

So the next day, once again they were waiting for John to arrive with the trailer bringing Sara back to them.

John unloaded her and, while Cass held her head, he checked her all over for any injuries.

'Is she all right?' asked Cass anxiously.

John went back to the near foreleg to run his fingers down the inside again. 'It feels a bit hot here,' he said. 'Just run her up and down for me, would you. Leave her head loose.'

Cass took the lead rope and led Sara away from him. As she trotted back towards him, John could see her head dipping unmistakably as the sound leg came to the ground.

'Well, you'd better rest her for a week,' he said. 'Have you got a garden hose? Good. Twenty minutes, morning and evening, run some cold water over the tendon to get the swelling down. I don't think it's all that serious, but if she's not all right at the end of the week, I should get a vet to look her over.'

'Poor Sara,' Cass said, her arms round Sara's neck.

'Where's your sister today, then?' John asked.

'She's in bed, the doctor came and said she'd got mild concussion. It happened when she fell off Sara.'

'How did that happen?' John asked. Cass told him what had happened, then added, 'It was a very high wind yesterday.'

'Aye, that often turns a horse scatty. Another point to keep in mind is that Sara's been used to company and now, being on her own, she probably gets a bit excited seeing some others of her own kind.'

'Oh dear. You think she's lonely, then?' said Cass.

'Wouldn't you be? They like company, horses do.'

'Well, we'll just have to get another pony!' said Cass, grinning.

After John had left, Lissa came down and they made

a big fuss of Sara. Cass fetched her some pony-nuts in a bucket from the ample supply in the feed-room, where they also kept a dozen bales of hay and straw.

It was hard to believe that Sara really was safely back in her own field, but at last they left her to go back to the house. Mrs Tallis was furious that Lissa was out of bed and sent her straight back upstairs.

'But I feel all right,' Lissa protested.

'The doctor said two or three days at least. Off you go!'

The only good part about it all was that Lissa had to have two days off school.

Eleven

The following weekend Cass got a letter. This was an unusual event, and because they all wanted her to open it right away, she decided not to, but took it up to the perch in the chestnut tree after breakfast to read in private. It said:

Dear Cass,

It was lovely to get a letter from you. I think about you and Lissa a lot. Saturday morning was murder this week, I overslept and Kerry did not turn up at all and we were late for the ten o'clock ride. Mrs Addison was in a temper and shouted at everyone, especially me for being late. She said if you are not on time there is no point coming at all. It was awful. We do miss you on Saturdays, it all seems such a scramble. We were cleaning tack till half past eight, Mummy was livid as they were going out and I was baby-sitting. It is not nearly as much fun without you. Tell Lissa Merlin is pining. No one can do anything with him. He keeps refusing at the jumps. He still stands at the end of the drive in the mornings, waiting. If there is any chance of you coming to visit, Mummy says you can stay with us for a few nights. I hope you like your new home. How lovely having your own stables, Lucky you.

Write again soon.

Love from Pat.

Cass reread the letter several times, then she scrambled down from the tree and ran up to the house. Mrs Tallis was in the kitchen, a headscarf over her hair, her face covered in dust as she struggled to remove some ancient shelves from the wall.

'Oh, Cass, take this end will you,' she said.

'The letter was from Pat,' Cass said.

'Quickly, I'm going to drop it!'

Cass took the shelf and helped her mother lower it to the ground.

'Look, it's from Pat. You must read it.'

'Not now, darling. I'm busy.'

'You must.'

Mrs Tallis took the letter from Cass and read it briefly.

'Oh yes. That's nice. My sink unit's being delivered this morning and I have to clear everything out of the way in time.'

Shortly after that a lorry pulled up in front of the house. Mrs Tallis opened the door and showed the men where the kitchen was and the two delivery men started unloading a large cardboard box.

'I hope I'll be able to sort it all out,' Mrs Tallis said anxiously. 'Cass, the plumber will be coming to fit the new sink, which means the water will be turned off. Can you fill all the kettles and saucepans you can find and make sure you put the lids on. There'll be a lot of dust.'

Cass filled the pans, impatiently hopping from one foot

to the other, groaning to herself because the water ran so slowly. When the last lid was on she went to look for Lissa.

Lissa was in her room, making a papier-mâché model of a horse. She had made the wire frame, pasted pieces of paper on to make the basic outline, and was now delicately moulding on tiny bits of paper to form the muscles around the shoulder and quarters.

'Who is it?' Cass asked.

'That depends,' Lissa said.

'Oh what?'

'Who it looks like. I'd like it to look like Merlin.'

'That reminds me, do you want to read my letter now?' asked Cass.

'Who is it from?'

Lissa's fingers were covered with paste. She wiped them on the bedspread.

Cass handed it over and watched Lissa's face anxiously. She wasn't at all sure how Lissa would react. Lissa read the letter in silence, then handed it back to Cass without a word.

'At least they miss us!' Cass said.

'I suppose they let those Dawson girls try to jump him. Well, I'm glad Merlin's got enough sense not to put up with it,' Lissa replied.

'It would be nice to go and visit them, wouldn't it,' Cass persisted.

'Not really. I don't see the point. Anyway, we can't afford it.' Lissa turned back to the model, but after a minute or two she lost interest.

'Shall we take Sara up on the hill?' Cass suggested.

'I don't feel like it. You can,' Lissa said. 'Can I read your letter again?' She carefully stood the model on the window-sill in the sun and put a newspaper over the bowl of paste to stop it going dry.

'If you want.' Cass gave it back to her.

There were now a lot of banging noises coming from the direction of the kitchen. The plumber must have arrived.

Lissa went down to the paddock and climbed the tree. She read the letter once, put it back in her pocket, and sat with her back against the huge trunk.

She saw Cass catch Sara, groom her, tack up and ride away. Then she shut her eyes and saw Merlin standing at the fence, as he always did, waiting. So he was still there, still missing her. She felt an ache in her chest and wondered how long it would be before she could forget him and he could forget her. She stared down at the deeply-grooved branches of the tree. She knew they had stood there for so many years, that all these emotions were just a speck of unimportance in the vast arena of time, but it didn't help.

If only they had been able to buy Merlin instead of Sara. If only she had known in advance that they might actually be able to buy a pony. But things never worked out that way. She felt instant remorse for being so disloyal to the gentle Sara, who was such a perfect pony. Guilt and despair and frustration.

She took out Cass's letter and read it and reread it many times until she could not see through the tears. Now it was smudged and Cass would be cross, so she put it away for ever, wishing she had never seen it.

Lissa suddenly felt the urge to go for a ride in the afternoon. This did not fit in with the weekend agreement, which was hacking in the morning, usually together, then schooling in the afternoons; Saturdays belonging to Cass,

Sundays to Lissa. Often they would practise one of five preliminary dressage tests that they had learned with Mrs Addison. Sometimes they would practise bending round some markers. It was not a great deal of fun without anyone to race against, although Sara was really good at flying changes, and also it was good to get the feel of her responding to the least possible touch on the rein and the lightest pressure of heel. So when at lunch-time Lissa said, 'Cass, could I have this afternoon, and you have tomorrow?' Cass protested: 'But it's my turn for schooling!'

'You did have her all to yourself this morning,' Lissa pointed out.

'Only because you didn't want to go!' Cass replied indignantly.

'Please.'

'Good heavens!' Mrs Tallis cried. 'You both ride every day, what can you possibly find to quarrel about!'

'Oh, all right,' said Cass, 'but you can do the tack, then.'

A couple of hours later Lissa was riding down the driveway towards the heath. When they reached the track that led between the cottages past Crawford's farm, on to the open hillside, Sara's stride lengthened and she lifted her head keenly. Somehow the fall Lissa had taken that day out on the hill had given her confidence rather than taking it away. Once the worst had happened, there seemed nothing left to worry about and, now that she knew Sara better, she felt sure it would never happen again.

A few hundred metres along the main gallops a small path forked to the left between banks of heather, swooped down into a copse where a small stream flowed and up the other side where someone had placed some brushwood across the path for jumping, and a succession of small logs. The path was well-beaten with hoofprints. Sara's ears went forward and she took the small course with enjoyment, leaping each obstacle smoothly and calmly. Out on the other side of the wood and along the ridge, between giant gorse bushes, was a clearing where they could stop to admire the view. At least, Lissa admired the view; Sara's head went down to crop at the short heath grass. A few metres away, a deer darted across the track, closely followed by another. The air was indescribably fresh, pure and alive.

Two riders were coming up from the valley. They were on ponies, a bay and a palomino. For a moment, Lissa's heart stopped. From a distance the bay was so like Merlin, in the jaunty way he moved, tossing his head and dancing a stride now and then. It wasn't Merlin, Merlin was much darker, anyway.

As they came closer, Sara whickered in welcome and Lissa recognised one of the riders, the one on the palomino. It was the girl with the brown pigtail, Angie, who was in Cass's class at school. Angie recognised Lissa at the same moment and waved. With her was a younger girl on the bay, which was much smaller than it had appeared from afar, only about 12.2 hands.

'Hello,' called Angie, 'on your own?'

'Yes. Cass was riding this morning.'

'This is my sister, Clare,' said Angie.

'Whereabouts do you live?' asked Lissa, thinking how marvellous it would be to have pony friends nearby.

'You can't see it from here, but it's the other side of that grey house.'

The two girls were wearing matching V-necked

jumpers in a dark red colour, with white shirts underneath. Lissa immediately felt slightly scruffy in the battered sweatshirt which she had hastily dug out from the bottom of her wardrobe.

'We're just going round the dip, then we're going home to do some jumping. Would you like to come along?' Angie suggested.

'Yes, please! But I've already gone round the dip, so I'll wait for you here.' Sara was disappointed to see the other ponies go cantering off without her and pawed the ground in frustration.

'It's all right,' Lissa reassured her, patting her neck. 'They won't be long.' She felt excitement rising in her and could not wait to tell Cass. She knew Cass would complain at it all happening without her but that could not be helped, it was such a stroke of good luck to find someone to ride with who lived nearby. When the holidays came, perhaps they could meet regularly at each others' houses and practise dressage tests and gymkhana games. The summer stretched ahead like some glorious, never-ending show, full of months upon months of good weather, riding, picnics and pony friends.

Soon the two girls were back, their ponies puffing slightly; they slowed to a walk and wended their way, with Angie in the lead, down into the valley and up the other side where the cluster of houses lay. Angie leaned forward to open a small gate on to a pathway and they all filed through. They waited while Clare battled with her fidgeting pony to close it.

'This is our place,' Angie told Lissa as they rode between paddocks, immaculate with heavy post-and-rails. 'Those are the jumps over there, but I'll show you the yard first.'

They rode into the prettiest stable-yard Lissa had ever seen, all whitewashed, with dark red doors and a fountain in the middle, feeding a horse-trough. Each stable had a proper name-plate, and at each corner was a hanging basket with ferns trailing from it. Tubs of conifers decorated the paving at intervals. Lissa sat open-mouthed and said in awe:

'It's beautiful.'

Angie laughed. 'It's not very horsy, but our mother's an interior designer, so she likes everything to look nice.'

Beyond the yard was a cream-coloured horse box.

'Daddy drives the horse box,' Angie explained. 'He hates shows really but he says he likes an excuse to sit and read all day. If he stays home, Mummy makes him do jobs around the house.'

'Aren't your parents at all horsy?'

'No, but Mummy thinks it impresses her friends, which is lucky for us. Let's do some jumping.'

In the paddock, a varied selection of jumps were already set up in a small course. There was a wall, about sixty centimetres high, which Angie said was only canvas so it would not hurt their ponies' legs if they knocked it. The first coloured poles were only about sixty centimetres off the ground, then there was a white gate, a double and a hog's back, all about seventy-five centimetres. Only the last one was higher at about one metre.

'Do you want to go first?' said Angie.

'If you like,' said Lissa, shortening her stirrups, in preparation.

'Can you hold Monkey while I do my stirrups? He won't stand still,' wailed Clare. Angie grabbed the pony's reins with her left hand and gave a quick jerk, and for a moment the pony stood still.

Sara's ears were pricked and Lissa was sure she was smiling. She pranced sideways and started to pull as they approached the first jump, so Lissa turned her aside into a circle and after cantering round twice Sara settled down into a smooth stride and Lissa popped her over the first one. She was delightfully comfortable to jump. Lissa felt in perfect balance with just the right tension on the reins. They took the whole course smoothly and calmly up until that last jump, then Lissa felt her confidence falter as she had never jumped anything quite that high before. Sara's ears flicked back questioningly and she came to it all wrong, put in an extra stride, jumped too close and hit it.

'Hard luck. It was super up till then,' called Angie.

Lissa jumped off with Sara's reins looped over her arm and set up the jump again.

Clare went next and did a clear round. Her pony was very keen and obviously born to jump. His little black legs flashed round the course, leaping everything with room to spare.

'She rides incredibly well,' said Lissa to Angie, thinking with envy that Clare could not be more than a year older than Ginny, and yet she had a naturally easy style that she could not fault.

'Makes you sick, doesn't it?' said Angie cheerfully. Her own pony, who was called Tulip, picked her way disdainfully round, hesitating slightly at each jump and hitting three of them. It was obvious that Tulip did not particularly like jumping and was more of a show pony as she moved so elegantly with her creamy mane and tail flowing like silk.

'She's won lots of rosettes for showing,' Angie said as they pulled up, 'but Monkey is hopeless at showing. He's too naughty. Once he bit the judge. I think it's all too slow for him, he likes action. He'd make a super hunter but Mummy won't hear of it, she's against blood sports. She's right, of course.'

After that, Angie said that if Lissa would hold her reins, she would put all the jumps up a bit and they would do it again, only they would leave the last one at the same height.

Sara sailed around the course again, and this time managed to clear the last one as well. Clare did the same.

'Could I ride Sara?' asked Angie. 'I don't like to make Tulip jump when she hates it so.' Lissa jumped off at once, glad of the chance to return a favour, and Angie got up on Sara.

It was soon obvious that Sara was not comfortable. Angie seemed to ride a little stiffly and her hands were not very giving. Sara took the first three jumps, tossing her head a little, but after a jab in the mouth kept her head too high and brought down three jumps in a row. Angie looked depressed.

'I don't know what I'm doing wrong,' she wailed.

Lissa was torn between keeping her mouth shut and upsetting her new friends by telling Angie what she was doing wrong.

'Can I try again?' Angie asked. Lissa hesitated. She did not want Sara upset, especially when she was jumping so well.

'Yes, all right,' she said.

At the first couple of jumps the same thing happened, and then Sara refused and ran out, highly indignant. Lissa was alarmed. 'Perhaps Sara's done enough,' she said anxiously.

'Would you like to try Tulip?' Angie suggested.

'Yes, please,' said Lissa. She got up on Tulip and let the stirrups down a hole. She felt her stride falter at the first jump and her head turned aside, looking for a way out, but Lissa used her legs strongly and forced Tulip over, who was so surprised at having a free head that she sailed over the other jumps without protest.

'She doesn't hate jumping at all. It's the way you ride her,' Clare said tactlessly.

Lissa felt her face go bright red and glanced at Angie, who looked very upset. They changed ponies without

123

speaking and Lissa had a horrible, sinking feeling that she had gone too far and everything was spoilt. If only she had not ridden Tulip.

They all left the paddock, shutting the gate behind them, and at the yard, as they were about to part company, Angie turned and said, 'Shall we ride again tomorrow?'

Lissa's heart leapt. 'I'd love to. Only it's Cass's turn.'

'I'd really like your help with my jumping,' Angie said.

Relief flooded through Lissa. 'I know, I can get Mummy to drop me round in the car, and Cass can hack over.'

Angie smiled. 'See you tomorrow, then.'

Lissa rode home on a rosy cloud of happiness. Along the ridge the sun was dipping below the horizon, casting long shadows behind the trees, and in the copse it was almost dark. Even the thought of Cass's fury at her long absence could not spoil the marvellous time she had had.

'It's just not fair!' Cassandra raged. 'Not only using up my riding time and wearing Sara out, you take off with my friends as well. I shall never forgive you.'

'I've arranged for you to meet her tomorrow,' Lissa replied, 'I'm going to ask Mummy to take me over in the car. You should see their stable-yard, it's brilliant.'

'Well, it's still not fair.'

'Life is never fair.'

'What are you so pleased about, anyway?' Cass asked.

'Angie wants me to help with her jumping. No one has asked me for help before, it must mean I'm getting better. We both are,' said Lissa.

'But we still need riding lessons,' Cass replied.

'I know, but even so, all the things Mrs Addison used

to tell us about hands and everything, it all makes sense now. It just proves what Mummy always says, that nothing you learn is ever wasted, sooner or later you come to use it, even if it takes years.'

'Mrs Addison did use to shout a lot, though,' Cass reminded her.

'I expect it was frustrating for her to keep telling people how to do things when they never did it. If only . . .'

'If only what?'

'I was thinking about Merlin. He's so young, and he still needs an awful lot of schooling. I just used to ride him, but now I bet I could really improve him. Nobody else is going to bother; Mrs Addison doesn't have the time. Eventually he's going to be spoilt, if he isn't already.'

'You still miss him?' asked Cass.

'More than ever. Don't you?'

'No more than all the others. Not now we've got Sara. You'll get over it,' said Cass, not looking at Lissa as she spoke. 'We'll have another pony one day, and we can look out for one that's just like Merlin.'

Lissa didn't even bother to answer. They both knew that nothing could ever take the place of a lost pony.

Twelve

It was a Saturday afternoon. Sara was standing patiently on the cobbles, allowing Lissa to wash and dry each of her hooves in turn in preparation for oiling. Cass was attempting to plait. Angie and Clare, who had come over for the day, were working on their ponies as well. Angie was sponging off stable stains, and Clare was trying to tidy up Monkey's rather frenzied-looking mane. It was just a practice-run, to make sure they could get ready for a show on time. On Sunday they were all going over to Angie's to practise jumping, because Angie's mother had invited the whole family to lunch.

'We'll have to learn to be quicker than this,' Lissa remarked, 'otherwise we'll never make it to a show in time.'

'We could do it the day before, and keep Sara in overnight,' Cass suggested.

'I don't think the plaits would last too well,' Lissa said, looking dubiously at the one Cass had just finished, where obstinate wisps of black mane refused to be restricted, and two earlier plaits were swelling ominously, about to burst out of their elastic bands. 'I think you'll have to work closer to the neck, Cass.'

'There'll soon be more elastic than hair,' complained

Cass. 'Poor Sara, isn't she patient.' She looked fondly into the huge dark eyes, so kind and trusting. 'I can't believe our luck, finding a pony like this. Mrs Beech could have asked twice as much.'

'Yes, but she wanted Sara to have a good home, and she's not all that fast after all,' Lissa replied.

'But she makes up for it by being careful,' Cass retorted. 'She never puts a foot wrong, do you, darling?' She put her arms around the pony's neck and pressed her face into the soft white fur.

'Careful,' said Lissa, 'you nearly undid one of your plaits.'

'Well, that's the best I can do for now. I shall have to practise every day till I can do it really well,' said Cass. 'Come on, everyone, I'm starving. Let's go and see if tea's ready.'

'I give up, I can't do anything with this mane,' Clare said.

Angie stood back admiring Tulip's damp but gleaming coat.

'Wait for me,' she said, 'I've just got to dry off a bit. Can you give me a hand?'

Everybody groaned, but they all went to fetch handfuls of hay to make into wisps for rubbing down.

As it was lovely warm June weather, Mrs Tallis had laid tea out in the garden, and presented them with a delicious looking spread of cakes and sandwiches.

'What shall we do now? asked Clare, when they had finished eating.

'I'm too full to do anything,' Angie said, leaning back in the grass and closing her eyes. 'I really shouldn't have had that last cake.'

'We could play hide-and-seek,' said Ginny hopefully.

No one ever seemed to have the time to play with her any more.

'It's a good idea,' said Clare. 'There are lots of places to hide. Shall we?'

Angie opened one eye. 'In the house or out?'

'Both, it will make it more interesting,' Clare put in.

'Who's going to be It?' asked Cass, coming round to the idea.

'Not me. I want to hide,' said Clare. Her face lit up. 'I've just thought of somewhere brilliant. You'll never find me.'

Cass went to fetch some playing cards from the house.

'Everyone take a card, and the lowest is It,' she said.

Angie and Lissa both drew threes, but the others had higher cards, so the two of them had to draw again. This time Angie had the lowest and, looking down at her watch, she said:

'Right. You've all got five minutes,' and she shut her eyes.

There was an immediate scuffle as they made off in all directions. At least one person could be heard thumping up the stairs, whilst others ran round the side of the house, feet scrunching on gravel.

Lissa and Cass both headed for the chestnut tree, then Cass veered left towards the shed. They both saw Clare waiting, a huge smile on her face, until they were both out of sight; Ginny had already disappeared.

For a long time nothing happened. Angie went upstairs and found Ginny first of all, and that took some time because there were so many hiding places. Lissa was found very soon after because Angie caught a glimpse of her red jumper high up in the tree.

Then Angie searched the stable-yard. She looked everywhere; behind the hay-bales, in the feed-bins, the shed, in the hedges, the bushes, and then went back to the house again. Finally, Cass was found behind a chair in the living-room.

'Cheat!' cried Angie. 'You weren't there to begin with.'

'I know. Still, it makes it interesting, doesn't it?'

'But where's Clare? I've looked everywhere.'

'You can't have,' replied Lissa.

'But I have.'

'Well, let's all look.'

They combed the house once more, searching every room, every corner, every cupboard. They scoured the garden again, front and back. They looked in every tree and bush, the orchard, the field, and the stable-yard, and at last gathered in the back garden, thoroughly puzzled.

'Where can she be? She's absolutely vanished.'

'She said we'd never find her,' Cass reminded them.

'Well, she'll have to come out sooner or later,' said Angie, sounding tired and cross. They wandered disconsolately towards the house, not knowing what to do next.

A door slammed hard, the sound echoing across the yard, and then footsteps crossed the stable-yard and Mr Hennessy came around the corner.

He shot a black look in the general direction of the girls, climbed into the red car and slammed the door. The engine obediently sprang to life, he fastened the seat-belt and the car leapt forward. That was when Clare appeared, her frantic face pressed up against the rear windscreen.

They watched in stunned silence as the car vanished round the side of the house. The next moment there was a long, terrified, high-pitched scream, the sound of wheels skidding on gravel and a crashing noise, which can only be described as the sound of a car going into a holly bush.

As they raced round to the front they were in time to see Mr Hennessy, his face white with rage, climbing out of the middle of an enormous holly bush where the bonnet of his car was buried, fling open the back and haul the hysterical Clare out on to the grass. Still screaming, she tried desperately to escape, but he hung onto her, lifting her bodily off the ground as she kicked and scratched in her efforts to get free.

'What the hell do you think you're doing, playing about in my car? And what are you screaming for? Shut up!' He was beside himself with rage. They thought he was going to kill her.

Mrs Tallis came running out of the front door and stood watching the scene in amazement.

He let Clare go then and she ran back sobbing to the others.

'Why do you allow them to play in my car!' he shouted. 'The stupid girl suddenly screamed in my ear, I could have had a heart-attack; no wonder I lost control. Look at it! And I've only just had the paintwork done.'

Then Mrs Tallis did a dreadful thing. She started laughing. Of course, she said she was sorry and tried desperately to stop, but it was too late. The children looked at her open-mouthed, and Mr Hennessy lost the last tattered shreds of his self-control.

'You're all mad!' he shouted. 'What on earth am I doing here! You children are allowed to run riot, and,' he turned to Mrs Tallis, 'you're as bad as they are. I've had radios blaring right under me when I'm trying to think, I've had my car wrecked twice, I've had drains blocked . . .'

'Drains? I didn't know anything about that,' said Mrs Tallis.

'I've had water flooding the kitchen floor, but what's the point, I got it fixed myself. I decided you can't cope with your own problems, let alone mine . . .'

'How dare you say that!' Mrs Tallis said in a voice which was icy cold.

'Look, I came here with a job to do, and I just want to be left in peace to get on with it, so can you please keep them away from me. All of them.' He spoke more calmly now.

'Mr Hennessy, or whatever your real name is, this isn't going to work. I think it would be best if I gave you your money back and you found yourself somewhere else to stay.'

For a moment longer he stood there staring at her, then without another word he got back in the car, started it up and slowly backed out of the bush onto the driveway. He did not get out to inspect the scratches, but it seemed the branches had shielded the car from the main trunk so the impact was not as bad as it might have been. He drove away without a backward glance.

'Mummy!' Lissa ran to her mother and took her hand. She could feel her mother trembling. 'Where will you get the money?' she whispered. Mrs Tallis hugged her and went back into the house, the children following meekly.

'Now, what *did* happen?' Mrs Tallis asked.

'Well, we were playing hide-and-seek,' said Ginny.

'I knew they would never think of looking for me there. I was hiding on the floor in the back of the car all the time!' said Clare, her courage slowly returning.

'Well, that was extremely stupid,' said Mrs Tallis. 'Now, you heard what he said. Just keep away from him.'

'I wonder what job he's talking about,' Cass mused. 'He has a lot of equipment in the cottage and he's awfully anxious for no one to go near him.'

'Perhaps he's printing money or something,' Clare suggested. She was over the worst of the shock now and was beginning to think it all was a great adventure.

'But why is he out so late every night?' Lissa reminded them.

'He could be a burglar,' suggested Angie. 'There have been a lot of robberies over the last few weeks. The police said they thought it was a London gang when our house got broken into last year. Well, he could be hiding out here.'

'Maybe the cottage is full of stolen treasure!' Clare said in a loud whisper. 'We ought to tell the police about him.'

'Nonsense! This has gone far enough,' Mrs Tallis said firmly. 'He's a nuisance, but I'm sure he's not a criminal.

'How can you be sure?' asked Cass. 'He's awfully rude.'

'You can't arrest someone for that,' said her mother.

'Mummy, are you really going to tell him to go?' Lissa asked anxiously. 'You won't have to sell Sara, will you?'

'Whatever happens, we won't sell Sara,' her mother promised. She went back to her kitchen then and Angie was able to say what she had been thinking:

'I wish we could see in the cottage to find out what he's got in there.'

'You heard what Mummy said. Keep away from him,' replied Lissa anxiously.

'You said he never comes back till after midnight.'

'There might be a reward, if we could tell the police where to find him,' said Clare.

'I think I've had enough excitement for one day,' said Cass.

'Oh, come on!' cried Angie. 'What about you, Lissa?'

'Well, you heard what Mummy said . . .'

'They're scared!' exclaimed Clare. 'Come on, Angie, you and I will go.'

So in the end they all decided to go. To Lissa's relief they were unable to get the spare key which was in her mother's handbag, so it was just a simple expedition to climb the apple tree which overlooked the upstairs window and try to peer in. A net curtain made it impossible to see anything through the downstairs window.

Angie wanted to be the one to climb, she said they never had adventures like this at home. Cass gave her a leg-up on to the first fork and from there it was easy. The tree was an old bramley apple with solid, forked branches, but higher up it became less easy. To get close to the window-sill Angie had to work her way along a branch which wobbled from side to side, but by clinging to the one above she made it, and was able to grab the sill. At this precise moment they heard a car coming up the driveway fast.

Cass shrieked: 'It's him!'

Angie started, her fingers slipped and she went plunging down through several branches on to the grass bank.

'Are you all right? Quick, get up,' they all said at once. Angie had no idea if she was hurt or not, but even a broken leg would not have held her down just then. With Cass on one side and Lissa on the other she scrambled over the gate and through the hedge just as Mr Hennessy came across the yard.

'I thought you said he never comes back till after midnight,' Angie whispered.

'He doesn't usually.'

'Whatever have you done to yourself?' Mrs Tallis asked

when she saw Angie, who was covered with scratches and green streaks from the bark of the apple, and her hair and clothes were full of twigs.

'She fell out of a tree,' Clare said honestly.

'She . . .' Ginny opened her mouth to speak and someone clapped a hand over it. Fortunately Mrs Tallis was pouring out lemonade at the time so she had her back to Ginny.

'I'm all right. It's nothing,' said Angie, and everyone exchanged glances of profound relief.

It was time for Angie and Clare to retrieve their ponies from the stables and go home. After they had gone, Lissa wandered inside where her mother was washing-up.

'What are you going to do about him, Mummy?'

'If I had the money, I'd give it all back and tell him to go; this situation has gone on long enough. As it is, it's all spent, we don't have any choice. We'll have to put up with him a bit longer. Mind you, that silly Clare was asking for trouble. How could she do such a thing?'

'He was very frightening,' said Lissa, remembering.

'Of course, with a bit of luck he may decide he's had enough and go,' Mrs Tallis continued. 'Except that he looked awfully shocked when I told him to leave. Well, I'm sick of him, and I'm sick of his wretched car.'

Mrs Tallis stared at Lissa in a fury, and then slowly a smile came back to her face.

'I've just realised, he's made me really angry, *really* angry. Isn't that strange? Well, he can keep his anger, too; there's no reason for me to be upset.'

The following morning, Lissa opened the front door and found a large bundle in the porch. It was a dozen bunches of flowers wrapped in paper with a note attached, addressed to her mother. It said simply, 'Sorry.'

Thirteen

From the highest point of the downs you could see three counties and, one evening, that's where Lissa stood, with Sara's reins in one hand. She had loosened the girth to give Sara time to get her breath back from the long gallop up the slow rise. They had passed other horses on the way but Lissa was now firmly in control and rather enjoyed the battle of wills. Occasionally she let Sara have her way and follow some others for a couple of hundred metres, but never long enough for Sara to feel that she was in charge.

Spring had long given way to summer, the white may had faded away to more mellow colours and the tips of the distant grasses swayed in waves of dark purple seed. Everywhere was a sea of green bracken and white birches dotted with pines and sinewy oaks. White clouds raced across the sky and small rabbits ventured out alone to explore. One came almost to where she stood, staring at her curiously and without fear.

Lissa watched it for such a long time that she did not see the sky darken and vast slate-grey clouds storm over from the west, until the sun suddenly vanished and enormous drops of water fell on to her bare arms. Glancing up she saw the storm clouds and hastened to tighten

Sara's girth and leap into the saddle. By the time she was halfway down the hill it was raining steadily and there was only time to reach the cover of a cluster of trees on the next rise before the storm broke.

Torrential rain crashed down around the solid cover of the pines. Sara searched the bare peat earth for a blade of grass but there were only pine cones, shut tight against the wet.

Lissa stood watching the grey wall of water, hoping it would let up, but it went on and on. Suddenly she became aware that she was not alone; through the trees to her right, someone else was standing watching the rain. A solitary figure, looking unnaturally still and tense, hands in pockets. It was Mr Hennessy. Lissa stiffened, feeling very uncomfortable, but there was no way out. If he looked in her direction she would have to speak to him. He looked at her as reluctantly as she looked at him, then after a long hesitation he strolled over and ran his hand down Sara's neck.

'Nice mare,' he remarked, 'had her long?'

'A few days longer than you,' Lissa replied, and wondered whether or not that sounded rude.

He went on patting Sara's neck, as though he wanted to say something and didn't know how to say it.

'How long have you lived here?' he said at last.

'Only since April,' Lissa replied.

'Is your father away?' That was what he wanted to ask.

'He died five years ago,' Lissa told him.

'Oh.' He looked up at her. 'There's a lot for your mother to do on her own,' he said.

'Well, we all help a bit.'

'I know.' Again he hesitated. 'I'm sorry I yelled at

you that day.' Lissa looked at him in amazement and muttered:

'It's all right. It was our fault.'

'Only partly. It was only because I was working on something, and when I've got a train of thought going I get mad when someone breaks it up. You two avoid me like the plague now, don't you?'

'But you said . . . well, Mother told us not to bother you. And . . .' the words came into her head and simply fell out, '. . . you always seem angry.'

'Do I? Well, not always.'

'You seem angry now. You were angry the first day you came to see the cottage.'

'No, I wasn't' he said and seemed genuinely puzzled.

'Yes you were. There's a big black cloud over your head, it's like electricity, telling people to be careful.' Lissa could hardly believe she was saying these things.

He looked at her, thinking about it.

'It's not anger. I've just got a lot on my mind.'

'It's as if you hate everybody and it's eating you up, like rust.'

His eyes widened then, and suddenly he turned away. Lissa felt frightened, as if by breaking into his reserve she had released the flood-gates of his rage and it was now about to envelope her.

There was a long, tense silence, broken when Mr Hennessy coughed.

'Out of the mouths of babes . . .' he said.

'I'm not a baby,' Lissa said, although she wondered if perhaps it would be safer to be one.

Mr Hennessy began to walk away from her and, at the boundary of trees, he returned, pacing backwards and forwards.

'It can't be that simple,' he said.

'What can't?' Lissa asked, but he was lost in his own thoughts and did not reply.

At last the barrage of rain lessened, the enormous hiss died down to a patter and finally ceased. Lissa mounted again, glad to be released.

'Well, goodbye,' she said cheerfully, and getting no answer, cantered joyfully down the splashy turf back to the track leading to the farm.

'Thank goodness,' her mother said when she walked in through the kitchen door. 'Where were you? I thought you'd drowned in all that rain.'

'Under some trees. It was quite dry,' was all Lissa said.

Mrs Crawford was sitting at the table, drinking coffee. She smiled at Lissa and Lissa smiled back. She did not look a bit like a farmer's wife was expected to look. Alison Crawford was slim and rather pale, with jet-black hair pulled back into a pony-tail. She did make lovely farm-house teas though, scones and fresh-whipped cream with home-made blackberry jam. The family had been over to tea a couple of times now, and Mrs Crawford often called in to see Mrs Tallis, bringing a tray of big brown eggs, or something from the dairy.

Lissa nearly mentioned her encounter with Mr Hennessy, but, for some reason, she didn't. She felt uneasy, and realised it was because she had not truly left Mr Hennessy behind on top of the hill; she was still half in and half out of his troubled world.

After supper Lissa went up to her bedroom to work some more on the papier-mâché model. The neck needed more weight, but it was shaping up nicely. If she could find some kind of black shiny string for the mane and tail, it would be a fair likeness. Then she remembered Cass's brown envelope with Merlin's own black hair inside it. With rising excitement, she carefully took it out of her treasure box and laid the precious strands on the floor. There was enough for the mane and forelock, as well as a lovely thick tail. How to fix it on was rather a problem until she decided to glue it to a flat strip of paper, then cover this with another layer of paper and paste.

Lissa was so engrossed in what she was doing that she hardly heard the car drive round the house and draw up at the cottage.

Cass came running into her room.

'Mr Hennessy's got some visitors,' she cried.

'Oh?' Mr Hennessy had not had any visitors since the second day after he moved in. 'What are they like?'

'I couldn't see. There were two of them, and they were carrying large black bags. Do you think they're part of a gang?'

'Did they say anything?'

'I couldn't hear. He opened the door and they went straight in. They're still there. Do you think they're planning something? Perhaps we ought to tell the police.'

'Don't be silly. What could we tell them?'

The girls raced downstairs and crept through the gate in the hedge, intending to listen, but they were too late. The visitors were already leaving and Mr Hennessy was with them.

'The car number! We should have got the car number,' cried Cass, jumping up and down as the car roared away up the hill.

'But we don't know,' said Lissa.

'Lissa!' cried Cass impatiently.' You're the one who

thought he was so suspicious. Why don't you want him caught?'

'I don't think he can be up to anything like robberies and things. I don't think he's all that bad really.'

'Since when?'

'I don't know,' Lissa said reluctantly.

'But he must be up to something.'

'I'm sure Mr Hennessy can't have anything to do with the robberies,' said their mother at breakfast the next day. He's been so much nicer lately. He even cut the hedge on Tuesday. And have you noticed, he doesn't stay out so late now? He seems to go out walking a lot more.'

'Mr Hennessy's not a robber,' said Ginny. No one took any notice of her, and she smiled as she helped herself to another slice of toast.

When Mrs Tallis drove them all home from school that day, a police car was waiting in front of the house. Another robbery had taken place the night before. A jeweller's family had been tied up and the jeweller himself was made to drive the thieves to his shop, where they took everything of value, including the entire contents of the safe. The police were now conducting a house to house search, asking every single person whether they had seen anything unusual, any stranger in the area, or any cars parked in unusual places.

Cass looked at Lissa, who looked at her mother.

'What is it?' the policeman asked, looking at them all intently.

'It's Mr Hennessy,' said Cass. 'I'm sure he's . . .'

'He's our tenant,' Mrs Tallis broke in. 'He might have seen something. You could ask him. It's through there.' She pointed the way, and the two policemen marched off through the gate in the hedge.

They were there for ages. Cass and Lissa sat in the window seat of the living-room for over an hour, expecting at any moment that the policemen would return with Mr Hennessy in handcuffs.

When they did return, it was without Mr Hennessy. One of them looked over solemnly at the two eager faces in the window, and touched the side of his nose with one finger and winked, then they got in the car and drove away.

'Whatever did that mean?' said Cass, bewildered.

'Goodness knows.'

'Well,' said their mother, 'now you can stop worrying and leave it to the police.'

That night Lissa dreamed she was in a small boat on a black sea and a great sea-monster kept appearing and trying to swallow the boat, but fortunately it never did.

Fourteen

The next morning, after breakfast, Lissa and Cass went to the stable-yard to paint three old scaffolding poles which Greg had brought for them earlier in the week. They had been lying around his brother's building yard and were no longer needed. Lissa glanced nervously up at the windows of the cottage as they tiptoed across the cobbles but Mr Hennessy was not to be seen.

It was fun painting the poles, sitting in the old harness room because it had been raining in the night and the yard was wet. Lissa carefully measured and marked five sections with a ruler and a felt tip pen, then both girls set to work with the white paint, filling in the middle and each end, leaving two blank spaces to be filled in with red the following day. Lissa said this would give them a centre to aim at when jumping. It was while they were working silently and in deep concentration that they heard small, determined footsteps crossing the cobbled yard towards them.

Cassandra looked out and saw Ginny advancing, not towards them but towards the yellow door of the cottage. She knocked at the door, it was opened, and in she went, without looking to right or left.

'Good grief!' Cass exclaimed.

'What?' asked Lissa, wiping her hands on a cloth.

'It's Ginny. She's just gone into the enemy camp. What can she be doing!'

'On her own?'

'Yes.'

The two girls looked at each other in amazement.

'Do you think we ought to go and rescue her?' cried Cass.

'Perhaps she has a message from Mummy.'

'She wouldn't have gone right in,' Cass persisted.

Lissa's face was creased with anxiety. 'We could go and tell Mummy,' she said.

'We might be too late! She might be murdered!'

'Not very likely,' Lissa muttered. She did not know what to do. Suddenly she made up her mind.

'Where are you going?' Cass asked.

'Where are *we* going?' Lissa corrected her. She felt a thrill of fear as she walked uncertainly across the yard to the lion's den. The yellow door was firmly shut. There was no sound of voices. She looked at Cass, then lifted her hand and knocked at the door. There was a long silence, then heavy steps could be heard descending the stairs. Mr Hennessy himself was coming to the door.

Lissa felt numb with apprehension. The door opened, and Mr Hennessy stood there, looking perfectly ordinary and natural, as though nothing unusual had happened. Lissa did not know what to say. Her mouth opened but nothing came out. It was Cass who spoke.

'We saw Ginny come in here!' Her voice was accusing.

'That's right,' he replied, staring back at her without any expression on his face at all. Then a broad smile came over his face and without another word he stood back and opened the door wide, pointing with one arm toward the stairs.

Lissa looked into the little room across to the open stairs, then she ran, with Cass close behind her, up two, three steps at a time. At the top they stopped to stare through the open doorway.

On one side of the room Ginny sat at some kind of keyboard, oblivious to the world as she concentrated on the sounds created by her fingers. She was playing with both hands some music from a piece of paper propped up in front of her. It was not printed, but hand-written on a sheet of music-paper.

All round the instrument were wires and boxes and speakers, piled up on top of each other. Next to Ginny's was another, much larger, with two keyboards and rows of knobs and buttons. Beyond that, a machine the size of a dining-table with row upon row of different coloured switches, hundreds of them. More speakers, large round reels, a television screen. The whole room was packed with equipment. Under the window was a desk and a chair piled high with books and papers.

Ginny glanced up, saw them, and scowled; her fingers faltered slightly, then she carried on with determination. Lissa wondered what had become of all the furniture so painstakingly carried up the stairs and arranged for the new tenant, then realised she must have passed it all in her headlong flight across the lower room. Only the wardrobe remained, squashed in a corner behind a speaker.

Ginny finished her piece and turned to them, her hands smugly folded on her lap. 'Mr Hennessy is teaching me to play the piano,' she announced. 'Mr Hennessy is my friend.'

He had walked over to the chair and sat down, looking highly amused.

'And,' said Ginny, 'Mr Hennessy wrote this tune especially for me. It's called "Ginny's Tune".' The two girls walked over to her and saw that the title of the piece was as she had said it was.

'Start from the top. Play it again,' Mr Hennessy suggested.

'Well, I don't know. I don't like people listening.'

'It's a good habit, right from the start, playing in front of people,' Mr Hennessy told her. 'Otherwise, if you practise by yourself for ever, you find you can't do it with other people around, and there is no point in that.'

'All right, then.' Ginny put her fingers carefully on the keys, looked hard at the music, and played. It was a pretty piece, in spite of the parts where her fingers hesitated over a difficult interval, or where there were several notes to play at the same time. Even so, Lissa and Cass were astonished.

'How many lessons have you had?' Lissa asked.

'About six or seven. And Mr Hennessy lets me come and practise, only then I have to turn the speakers off and use these headphones so I don't disturb him. Look.' She turned a switch and picked up the headphones for them to listen, then played a few bars more so that they could hear.

'How often do you come and practise?' Cass asked.

'Nearly every day. Only sometimes Mr Hennessy doesn't want to be bothered and I have to go away.'

Lissa knew vaguely that she ought to apologise to Mr Hennessy, or at least to feel embarrassed about their abrupt visit, but she was too fascinated by all she saw to think about it. 'What's this?' she asked, pointing to the large instrument with the hundreds of switches on it.

Mr Hennessy got up from his chair.

'That's just the desk where I control the sound on the different tracks. This is a drum machine, this is . . .'

'What is it all for?' Cass asked.

'Mr Hennessy writes music. He writes music for films,' Ginny said in a voice which implied that they were awfully stupid not to know. 'Do you want to hear some of it?'

Without waiting for an answer, Mr Hennessy pressed a switch and a reel started running.

'Put the picture on with it,' Ginny told him, so he switched on the television screen as well and, at a certain point, pressed a button to start the picture. The first few minutes were just titles and names which Lissa did not take in because she was listening to the music and watching Mr Hennessy at the same time. She found it so amazing that the beautiful haunting sounds should have been created here, in this room, while they had all been carrying on as normal outside, completely unaware that this was happening. She shut her eyes for a while, hearing the white ghosts of may-blossom and the turbulent currents of air, carrying storm clouds across the crests of the hill.

He was standing at the window, staring out as the music played. Lissa thought that she had never heard anything so lovely. It was a completely new experience. Ginny sat on her stool, watching the screen enraptured, as the story began about a family living in the mountains. Cass sat cross-legged in front of the screen.

'I think it works all right,' Mr Hennessy said. 'It's the best thing I've done yet. I don't think it would have happened anywhere else but in this room, with this hill in front of me. Do you like it?'

'Yes,' Lissa said. 'Is it finished?'

'Two days ago,' he replied. 'Sam Heffler came down with the producer and picked it up.'

'The men with the black bags?'

'You saw them? Yes, we all went out to celebrate at the Half Moon.'

'The Half Moon?'

'The pub in Chaseford, down by the river. I don't suppose you children notice these things, but I know it rather well.'

'We've never been down to the river,' Lissa said. Her head felt like a traffic-jam of all the thoughts and fears she had experienced in the last three months.

'Is my lesson over?' asked Ginny, disappointed.

'I'm afraid so, but we can probably fit another one in tomorrow.'

The children trooped out, Cass first, followed by Ginny. At the last, Lissa turned to face him, wanting to say she was sorry, but not knowing how. No words came and she turned and ran after the others.

'Did you know Ginny was having piano lessons from Mr Hennessy?' Lissa asked her mother as she went in the back door. Mrs Tallis was standing at the sink preparing vegetables.

'I found out this morning.'

'Why didn't you tell me?' Lissa demanded, feeling betrayed.

'You weren't here and besides, Ginny wanted to keep it a secret to surprise everybody.'

'She's done that all right,' Lissa said, glaring with resentment at her younger sister who sat at the kitchen table swinging her legs and nonchalantly popping peanuts into her mouth.

'I think it's mean,' said Cass, 'to let us go on wondering what's going on in that cottage and all the time she's been going in and out of there.'

'Not *all* the time. Only for the last two weeks,' said Ginny, 'and it had to be a secret because if I told you, someone might have stopped me, and Mr Hennessy made me swear not to tell.'

'But why?' said Lissa. 'Why doesn't he want anyone to know what he's doing.?'

At that precise moment, in the extraordinary way that life has of conducting itself, there was a tremendous clattering of hooves in the kitchen yard and when Cass threw open the door, there was Angie, flinging herself out of the saddle, waving a newspaper and screaming:

'He's here, he's here in the paper, your Mr Hennessy. We know who he is.'

Clare, who was close behind her but who had the foresight to keep hold of Monkey's reins, made a grab for Tulip, and stood there holding the ponies while Angie came into the kitchen and laid her newspaper across the table, open at the second page.

Beneath a headline reading:

MYSTERY OF VANISHING MUSICIAN

was a fairly large photograph of Mr Hennessy, and below that a paragraph reading:

Alan Westwater, the musician and composer who disappeared three months ago, is still being urgently sought by friends and business associates. Mr Westwater discharged himself late one night from a London clinic where he was being treated for nervous exhaustion, and has not been heard of since. His doctor believes he may be suffering from amnesia . . .

'What's am – amnesia?' asked Ginny.

'Loss of memory,' Mrs Tallis said in a distant way.

There were a few more lines, giving details of his career, and asking for information from anyone who might know where he was.

For a time there was silence around the table. They were all quite stunned by the news.

'What should we do?' said Cass at last. 'Oughtn't we to tell someone.'

'No,' said Ginny. 'He doesn't want us to. That's just why he never told us in the first place.'

'It's a difficult situation,' said Mrs Tallis. 'I hate to

think of people worrying about him.'

'There must be a reason why he's hiding,' said Lissa. 'He certainly hasn't lost his memory.'

'It says he was suffering from nervous exhaustion,' Mrs Tallis mused.

'What does that mean?' asked Cass.

'It means a nervous breakdown. It means he was skiving,' said Clare from the doorway. 'My father says he wishes he could afford the luxury of a nervous breakdown sometimes.

'Don't be ridiculous, you shouldn't repeat things when you don't know what they mean. Nervous exhaustion comes from thinking too much. That's something you'll never have to worry about, Clare!' Mrs Tallis retorted with unusual sharpness. 'It says here he was in the middle of another concert tour when he became ill and went into the clinic. When he first arrived here he told me his doctor had ordered him into the country for rest and quiet. It was almost true.'

'Does your father know about Mr Hennessy?' Cass said to Angie.

'Well, we had to tell him something,' Angie replied. 'There we all were at breakfast, and my father was buried behind the *Guardian* as usual, and suddenly Clare screamed and pointed at the picture of Mr Hennessy on the outside of the paper. We had to tell him who it was because Clare made him spill his coffee and he was ever so cross.'

'So he knows,' said Lissa, not sure whether to be glad or sorry. 'What about your mother?'

'Oh, she was on the phone to her friends straight away. I expect she still is. But I made her promise not to give your address.'

'Thanks a lot!' said Mrs Tallis. 'Well, the first thing I'd better do is have a chat with Mr Hennessy and tell him what's happened. Then it's really up to him.'

'Mr Westwater,' Angie corrected her. 'That's his real name.'

'He'll always be Mr Hennessy to us,' said Cass.

'Does this mean he'll have to go away?' Ginny asked anxiously.

'Very likely, darling,' replied her mother. 'Which is a pity, I hate the thought of advertising for a tenant all over again.'

'We might get someone much nicer,' said Cass.

'We'll never get anyone as nice as Mr Hennessy. He mustn't go. Mummy, don't let him go.' Ginny suddenly burst into loud sobs, covering her face with her hands. Lissa was fascinated to see the tears actually reaching her chin and dripping on to the table. Everyone stared in shocked silence; Ginny was usually so self-contained and went about the house quietly amusing herself, so that nobody thought about her very much, except her mother, who now sprang to her side and put her arms around her.

'Mr Hennessy is the only one who let me have a piano to play. He's my friend.' Her voice, thick with emotion and broken by gasps of air, was quite shocking. Lissa felt overcome with guilt and realised how much she had been taken up with her own affairs since moving to the new house; that she never talked to Ginny the way she used to.

Gradually the sounds died down and Ginny became calm again. Her mother washed and dried her face and Ginny looked around her at the anxious faces with a slight smile on her face, enjoying the sensation of being the complete centre of attention.

'It's Mr Hennessy's birthday tomorrow,' she said.

'How do you know?' Cass asked.

'I asked him. I asked him how old he was,' said Ginny.

'How old is he?' Cass spoke, but Ginny looked at them all smugly in turn, knowing they were waiting for her answer.

'He's twenty!'

'Oh Ginny! He was lying to you.'

'He wasn't. He's twenty.'

'He didn't lie,' corrected their mother, laughing. 'He was joking. People joke about their ages sometimes, Ginny.'

'But he *is* twenty,' her mouth turned down in that special, comical way.

'No, dear.'

'So his birthday isn't tomorrow? I was going to give him a present.'

'Oh, I expect he was right about that, if that's what he said. If you want to give him a present, I think he'd be very pleased. It would be a nice way of saying thank you for the piano lessons,' Mrs Tallis said.

'I shall give him a present as well,' Lissa said, though she had no idea what she might give.

'Do you think he would like my painting of the view from the cottage window?' asked Cass. Her mother looked surprised.

'Are you sure you want to give that away?' she asked.

'It will remind him of the cottage when he goes back home,' Cass replied.

'I'm sure he'd like it,' said Mrs Tallis.

Soon after that Angie and Clare left for home, and Mrs Tallis went over to the cottage to tell Mr Hennessy what had happened.

Fifteen

It was almost dark, and the sky was coloured by swirls of smoke laced with red sparks. Everywhere was the delicious smell of wood-smoke from the bonfire as the debris burned, spitting and crackling. Now and then the wind changed direction suddenly, and everyone had to dive out of the way of the smoke. They all stood close, enjoying the warmth while Cass held the pitchfork, feeding the fire at intervals from a huge pile of cuttings. In the embers, some large, blackened potatoes were roasting.

Lissa looked back through the trees at the solid, dependable outline of the house. In the darkness the shabby frames were hidden, and only the reflection of the sparks in the window panes were visible. Mrs Tallis was carefully prodding the potatoes with a long skewer.

'I think these are done,' she said. 'Could you go and fetch some plates, Lissa.'

Lissa ran up to the house and piled a tray with knives and forks, plates, butter, a large bottle of ginger beer that she found in the larder, and some plastic cups. As she hurried back across the yard she did not hear the footsteps coming from the opposite direction, until she crashed into Mr Hennessy at the corner of the shed. Everything went clattering to the ground.

'I'm sorry,' she said, picking up a plate, which was unbroken.

Mr Hennessy began to help her, searching in the bushes for the pieces. Nothing was broken, just rather dusty.

'It's a good bonfire. Are you having a party?' he asked.

'Not really, just burning the rubbish.' Lissa remembered it was his birthday next day and had a feeling she ought to ask him to join them, but she didn't want to. The light from the fire glowed red on both their faces and reflected off the walls and windows. She counted the pieces on the tray. There was only a knife missing, but it would have to wait till daylight.

'I was thinking,' he said, 'about what you said that day up on the hill. I truly don't hate anyone, you know. I'm just preoccupied. Wrapped up in myself. I expect I'm very selfish. If it comes out as – as dislike, then I'm sorry, because it's not that at all.'

Lissa looked at him in surprise, and at that moment it was hard to remember why she had felt such hostility towards him.

'It's all right,' she said. 'I'm like that at school sometimes, only I don't get angry. I just go quiet. It's like looking through the window at people and not being able to get in.'

Above their heads the deep red sparks flew up into a sky so deeply blue it was electric.

'Isn't it beautiful!' she exclaimed.

'Beautiful,' he agreed. High above, the sparks faded to blend with the silver of the stars until they vanished altogether in the sky.

'Funny to think,' Lissa remarked, 'that we may have lived on one of those stars in another life.'

'How do you mean?' Mr Hennessy asked.

'Well, if our life-essence goes on forever, as it's supposed to, and the whole universe is all one, and we keep going on being born, and living, then not living for a while, we might just as well be born up there on another world as down here.'

'Doesn't that idea frighten you?' he asked.

'No, I should like to visit other places.'

He was silent for a moment, then said gravely, 'And where do we go when we die?'

'It's like a drop of water returning to the ocean. It's all in the book my father wrote. I'll ask Mummy if you can borrow it – that is if you'd like to.'

'You must miss your father very much.'

'When we moved,' Lissa said slowly, because she had never told this to anyone before, not even to her mother, 'I was afraid he wouldn't find us, so I wrote our new address on the wall in my bedroom, in the little alcove.'

'And did he find you?' asked Mr Hennessy, with deep interest.

'He didn't have to. I just know he's everywhere. When I look at his photograph now, it's almost like the face of a stranger, but it doesn't matter because he doesn't need that face any more.'

There was a deep silence between them, deeper than the sky. Then Mr Hennessy said, almost in a whisper, 'Thank you for telling me that.'

'Well, Mummy's waiting,' Lissa said, looking over to the fire, and she moved awkwardly away.

Mr Hennessy was left standing in the middle of the path, watching the sky, and when Lissa finally looked back he was still there, hunched up against the night, unmoving. Lissa felt a sudden chill go through her as she felt a sense of immense loneliness, and she realised that even if a lot of people were standing there with him, it would make no difference. He would still be different, alone. She shuddered at this thought and hurried back to the fire.

'Wasn't that Mr Hennessy over there?' Mrs Tallis said. 'You should have asked him over.'

'He's gone now,' said Cass. The space where he had stood was now empty, although the unease was still there.

Early the following afternoon, Lissa was once again knocking at the yellow door of the cottage. Cass wanted her to go over in the morning, but Lissa thought he might be grumpy first thing; she still felt a bit nervous.

There was no reply, as she half expected, although she knew Mr Hennessy was in there. He was most likely working, probably in one of his moods.

Lissa stood there, trying to summon up the courage to knock again and fighting the impulse to escape to the chestnut tree and forget the whole project on this lovely, sunny afternoon.

After what seemed like a very long time, a gruff voice barked out: 'Come on in, then.'

The voice came from upstairs, so she climbed the flight of stairs to the room above. He was sitting in an armchair at the open window with his blank face towards the hills, there was music-paper on his knees, also blank, and a pen hung from his lethargic fingers.

There was something running on the television screen, with the dialogue set at a very faint level. Lissa waited, feeling very awkward, sensing the tension in him like some great engine at full power but without the lever to release it. At length he gave a vast sigh, spun round in his chair and turned to face her with a polite smile.

She felt very nervous now and almost said sorry instead of 'Happy Birthday' as she thrust the package towards him.

He stared at it with a puzzled frown, then reached out and punched a button on the video. The film stopped.

'What's this?' He looked at Lissa with a piercing blue look, a look that seemed to see all her secrets. He took the package, felt it, just as an ordinary human being would, and untied the rather shaky knot. He took off the outer layer, then the red tissue, and finally uncovered the brown papier-mâché horse, complete with white star. Merlin.

It had taken a lot of soul-searching for Lissa to decide to give it away. Even now, she was not quite sure why she had done it. A lot of hard work and devotion was tied up in the model, as well as a lot of pain and despair. She had wanted to give something that was important to her though, because this might make up for all the bad things she had thought about Mr Hennessy.

She stared at the model as it lay in the palm of his hand, and he stared at it also, and then Lissa had a strange experience: quite suddenly, she completely understood Mr Hennessy's own pain and grief, perhaps just for that moment only. She could hardly breathe with the knowledge. Later, she remembered reading something her father had written about the act of giving; how it could open up channels for receiving, whether thoughts or ideas, respect, or even material things.

Mr Hennessy put the model down and opened the envelope to take out Cass's hand-painted birthday card. Lissa held her breath as he read the words: 'To dear Mr Hennessy. We wish you the happiest birthday ever, and a very happy life.' He stared at the card for what seemed an eternity, and then at Lissa. She began to go red and move from foot to foot. Perhaps he thought it was a very childish thing to do, perhaps he hated ornaments, perhaps he was still angry at the interruption. Then, to her absolute horror, one tear trickled out of the corner of his eye and made its way down the rough, grown-up face. Lissa turned instantly to flee, but Mr Hennessy said:

'No, don't go. I shall treasure these things always.'

'The horse is called Merlin,' Lissa told him.

'Why didn't Cass come with you?'

'We tossed a coin . . .' Lissa stopped, open-mouthed at her own words. Mr Hennessy threw back his head and laughed and laughed. She looked at him in fascination, never having seen him laugh before.

'Well, tell Cass I thank her very much. And what else are you holding?'

'Ah.' Lissa gently handed over the precious painting.

He removed the tissue and held it at arm's length between his two palms.

'Cass did this?' he said, almost unbelieving. He got up and went to the window to compare the reality. Everything had changed now, the blossom trees were green, the white may gone and the trees were dark with the rich green of summer, and part of the view in the picture was now blocked by foliage, the stark black branches covered with growing fruits, but the outline was unmistakable.

'That's quite remarkable,' he said. 'She's a very talented girl. I hope she takes it up as a career.' He propped the picture on top of the bookshelf and continued to gaze at it with obvious pleasure.

'I expect she will. I wish I could paint like that,' Lissa replied, looking at the picture with him and remembering the atmosphere of the first few days at their new home which the painting always managed to arouse in her. It was always surprising.

'Lissa,' he said seriously, 'with a soul like yours there is no need for pictures or music or anything else. These are only ways and means. You go straight to the heart of the matter. It's called life.'

'I don't know what you mean. Cass can go off and paint whenever she gets bored, I can't. Oh, I nearly forgot, Mummy has made you a cake. She said would you like to come over for tea? Or if you'd rather not, she'll send the cake over.'

'I think I'd like to come to tea.' He sounded surprised and pleased. 'On my birthday. Yes, tell your mother I'll come over. Run along now, I've got a bit of work to finish.'

'About five?'

Something had changed. Lissa knew as soon as she ran out of the yellow door and closed it that the visit was a success and things would never be the same again.

'What did he say?' asked Cass. Lissa hesitated, wondering how much to tell her and, for some reason unknown even to herself, decided to say nothing.

'He loved your painting. He thinks you're terribly clever and you ought to take it up for a living.'

Cass beamed. 'Did he really? Great! Wouldn't it be lovely to paint all day and never have to go to school.'

'He liked the card too, and the horse. He's coming over to tea.'

'Well, you'd better give me a hand,' said Mrs Tallis. 'Can you wash up while I start cooking?'

'I love this house,' said Lissa, picking up a cloth. 'It's a real home, more than our other house ever was.'

'I expect that's because you've been a part of it all,'

replied her mother. 'When you work on something, you feel much closer.'

Just after five o'clock there was a knock on the door. All three girls had been made to wash and put on clean dresses and brush their hair. It was the first time Mr Hennessy had been inside the house since his arrival. The outside was still very much as it had been when they moved in, although tidier, but the inside, at least at ground level, was completely transformed.

The hall itself was now alive with colour, with Mrs Tallis's collection of paintings now framed and hung, and Mr Tallis's books lining the walls from door to door, and flowers from the garden in every corner. The three children watched from the door as Mr Hennessy stopped to look at a small collection of oil paintings, about nine of them, opposite the stairs.

'You've got some Van Loocks,' he exclaimed. 'Where did you find them?'

'I bought them years ago, when I was still at art college,' Mrs Tallis said.

'But what a coincidence, I've been collecting some myself. You wouldn't think of selling a couple, I suppose?'

She laughed, not taking his question seriously.

'This house is so different on the inside,' Mr Hennessy said with admiration. 'It's so colourful.'

'I believe in starting with the core of a house,' Mrs Tallis replied. 'We haven't had the time or money to get around to the outside. We only moved in here a couple of weeks before you and the condition of it was appalling. As it is, there is still the kitchen to do and most of the upstairs.'

'What made you come here?' he asked, as she handed him a cup of tea.

'The house was given to us by my father-in-law, and quite honestly, we had nowhere else to go. As it is, things are turning out very well. The girls are happy with the stables, and we're gradually getting things under control. The worst problem now is some rot in the attic. We've had it patched up temporarily, but it has to be properly treated.'

Lissa was thinking that the house was a bit like Mr Hennessy himself, off-putting on the outside, but rather nice inside. They began talking about the place where they used to live, and Cass remembered Pat's letter.

'Do you think we might be able to go and see her one day?' she asked. 'I'd love to go and see all the ponies again.'

'It is a shame about Merlin, isn't it. Would you like to go back for a visit sometime, Lissa?' Mrs Tallis asked gently.

'Not particularly,' Lissa replied.

'But I thought you were fond of Merlin?'

Lissa's face froze in an effort to fight back the tears.

'She is,' Cass put in, making frantic gestures to her mother to change the subject.

Lissa was staring at a piece of pattern on the chair with such intense feelings that she knew for the rest of her life, whenever she saw that particular pattern, she would think of Merlin. She knew they were all looking at her, and felt her face go hot and red.

'Well, it's a long way and quite an expense,' her mother said. 'Now, who would like another piece of cake?' She was trying to take their attention away.

Mr Hennessy began to talk about Cassandra's painting. He was going to get it framed and hang it in his London studio to remind him of the cottage. He said it would inspire him whenever he got stuck on a piece of music.

'You must make sure Cassandra is properly trained as she gets older,' he said seriously. 'She really is very good.'

'If it's what she wants to do,' Mrs Tallis replied.

When they finished eating, Mr Hennessy insisted on helping to clear up.

'I told you the kitchen was a mess,' Mrs Tallis said, looking ruefully at the pile of cooking utensils which she had not had time to wash. Every spare corner was filled with boxes still unpacked because there was nowhere to put anything.

'You're not trying to do all this yourself, are you?' he asked.

'Of course,' she said. 'I'm quite capable of handling a screwdriver. I managed the sink unit, and now I'm putting up some shelves.'

'I shall help you. It's the least I can do.'

Mrs Tallis looked astonished. 'Well . . . all right then. Thank you.' Soon he was standing there with a drying-up cloth in his hands, looking quite comfortable in the middle of all the chaos, while Mrs Tallis washed-up and the girls helped stack things away. As they worked he told them a little about his own life on the road as a musician, the countries he had been to and the people he had met.

'Now everything is out in the open, how soon will you be leaving us?' Mrs Tallis asked.

'I haven't decided,' he said. 'I've got several trips to make, one to New York and another to Japan. I've got some work to do over there which will take a month or two.'

'But what about the clinic? Do you have to go back?'

Mr Hennessy smiled. 'No, I'm all right now. I just

needed a good rest. I've been working for three years without much of a break and then, just after the New Year, my sister died, which was quite a blow. I just wish I could have been there.'

Lissa remembered the conversation they had near the bonfire, and the expression on his face as he watched the sparks flying up among the stars. It all made sense now, and she felt deeply sorry. She wished she could be one of those people who always manage to find the right words at the right time. Instead, as she looked up at Mr Hennessy and met his eyes, it was as if he was reassuring her.

Later, he went over to the cottage to fetch a bottle of

wine to share with her mother, and after the girls had gone to bed he stayed on. Lissa could hear the murmur of their voices through the floorboards.

Sixteen

A few days later, Cass and Lissa were taking Sara out to the dell to practise some jumping. Angie and Clare were away on holiday although the term was not due to end until the following week. It was Lissa's turn to ride, and Cass was walking along behind feeling rather tired and grumpy.

'It's time we had two ponies,' she said.

'What?' Lissa called.

'I said, it's time we had two ponies. I'm sick of walking!' Cass yelled. Sara tossed her head at the disturbance and Lissa patted the smooth grey neck.

'It's all right, take no notice,' Lissa said. The tack felt slightly sticky because she had not bothered to clean it for a couple of days. She could remember the day Sara arrived, when she had vowed to herself to keep the tack and everything in spotless condition and to clean it every time it was used, just like Mrs Beech did. She stopped Sara, and dismounted to let Cass catch up.

'You can ride for a while.'

'Why? It's your turn.'

'It doesn't matter.' She watched Cass canter off, and followed in a leisurely way. There was a fallen log at the top of the dip, and she sat for a while as Cass went round the miniature course, trying to pace her take-offs accurately. Sara's neat black legs flowed in action like a dancer's, and Lissa watched her with pleasure.

She felt very strange this morning, as though something was different; and she did not know what it was. Mr Hennessy was busy working on the kitchen shelves with her mother helping him. Lissa wished they were not quite so friendly, although it was better than having to creep into their own stable-yard, feeling the hair rise on the back of her neck at the slightest sound. No, she did not feel Mr Hennessy was the cause of this strange feeling, though he might be a part of it. It was as though life was suspended in some way. Even the trees seemed to be holding their breath as if waiting for something to happen.

When they got back home, there was a strange car in the drive, a large white one with a smoky windscreen.

'Who can that be?' said Cass. They turned Sara out in the field, and Cass said she would clean the tack, so Lissa went up to the house alone.

In the kitchen, a tall, strange woman was talking to her mother and Mr Hennessy. She was very slim with shoulder-length, streaky, blonde hair, and her hands, long, thin and very brown, sparkled under the weight of countless rings and bangles. She wore a white suit with a black shirt and very high white sandals. She glanced over as Lissa came in the door, and her eyes registered instant contempt. Lissa was suddenly aware of the stains on her tee-shirt and her tousled hair. The woman was in the middle of saying something and, after a frown of annoyance at the interruption, she continued:

'But if you wanted to help, why didn't you just pay someone to come and do it? I've never seen you do manual work before, Alan. After all,' she added, 'you know you have to take care of your hands. Don't forget you have a concert next month in New York.'

Mr Hennessy and the stranger looked at each other. He opened his mouth to speak, then closed it again. Lissa saw an expression come over his face that she recognised. It was the feeling you get when someone puts a maths problem in front of you and suddenly you realise you have no idea how to do it. He shrugged. 'I wanted to do it. Believe it or not, Sylvia, I'm enjoying myself, And I hadn't forgotten about the concert.'

There was a brief silence, broken by Mrs Tallis:

'Can I offer you some coffee?'

Lissa noticed her mother's bruised and roughened hands and the tear in her jeans. There were streaks of black dust on her nose and down one side of her face. The woman glanced around the kitchen with distaste.

'I think that might be difficult right now. In any case, I have to get back to the office. I must talk to you, Alan. Perhaps you would walk me to my car.'

'Of course,' he said. Without a word she turned on her heel and left the room. Through the open window, their voices came quite distinctly.

'I'm sure I don't have to tell you how disappointed I am that you chose not to let me know where you were hiding,' the woman said in a voice that was hard and cutting. 'Even Brian and Sam told me they didn't know where I could find you, and I know that was untrue. After all the years of work I've invested in your career . . .'

'You made a very good living out of me, Sylvia. If you hadn't pushed me so hard, maybe I wouldn't have cracked.'

'I'm your agent, it's my job to push you. I made you what you are, then you disappear without a word. You even closed your bank account so no one could trace you.'

'I was ill, Sylvia. I warned you I was ill. You wouldn't listen. Three years without a break . . .'

'I'm not interested. Be in my office by Monday the third, or consider our contract cancelled. As for this score you've been working on, I'm not sure whether that's excluded in the terms of our contract. I'll have to consult the legal staff.'

'Oh, no,' said Mr Hennessy. 'I've already had it checked. That's one thing you can't get your hands on, Sylvia.'

'Well, don't let me down over the tour. The phone hasn't stopped ringing with people asking me are you doing it or not. Remember, Monday the third.'

Soon after they heard the car door slam, and Mr Hennessy's footsteps tramping back across the gravel.

'I'll carry on with the shelves, now,' he said.

'You don't have to,' said Mrs Tallis.

'I can't think of anything I'd rather do,' he said, and was soon drilling and banging so hard, Lissa thought the wall would fall down.

At Ginny's bedtime, Mrs Tallis told him to stop.

'I've come to a decision,' he said.

'What about?' she asked.

'I shall do this tour because so many people are involved and I can't let them down, but this will be the last. After that I shall get back to composing, it's what I enjoy most. So I want to keep the cottage on, even though it will be empty for a while. It's the only place I can get any work done. Is that all right with you?'

'It's all right with me,' said Mrs Tallis.

That means we get our rent and for the next few months the cottage will be empty, Lissa thought.

'I feel relaxed here,' he went on. 'It's a happy place to

be and I have you to thank for that. All of you.'

'We're glad to have been able to help,' said Mrs Tallis.

'And I'm leaving some of my equipment in the cottage,' he said. 'Ginny can go and use the piano whenever she likes, though it's not the same as a real piano.'

'We'll try to get her one soon,' said her mother. Lissa began to feel that she rather liked him, now that he was actually going. It would seem strange in the yard, knowing that the cottage was empty.

On Thursday night, Mr Hennessy came over to the house to say goodbye. His suitcases were packed, as well as most of the equipment he was to take with him, as he was leaving very early the next morning. He did not stay long. He shook hands solemnly with each of them in turn, but when he came to Mrs Tallis, he stopped and just looked at her. Glancing up, Lissa intercepted an exchange between them that made her look down again quickly, as though she were guilty of listening at doors. It was a look of such closeness that for a moment tears pricked her eyes. When she finally lifted her head again, Mr Hennessy's arms were round her mother in a great bear-hug, and on her mother's face a look of such happiness that Lissa did not feel left out at all. There was a smile wide enough to include the whole world.

'Excuse me, children,' he said with great good humour, 'but this has to last me for an awful long time.' Strangely enough, Lissa felt no resentment, no fear. Instead, it was like part of an inevitable pattern unfolding and to her surprise what she really felt was relief, like the finding of something lost.

Ginny was also watching, but with a scowl on her face. Frantically she pushed between the two of them. 'When I grow up, will you marry me?' she asked Mr Hennessy.

'When you grow up, I'll have long white hair. Will you still want me?' Mr Hennessy asked quite seriously.

'How do you know? You might go bald!' Ginny said.

Mr Hennessy clutched his head in horror. 'In that case, I should have to wear a wig, especially for you.'

'Ginny, don't be such a wally,' Cass cried, seizing her hand and jerking her away.

After he had gone, Mrs Tallis gave a deep sigh. 'I do hope he'll be all right,' she said.

Lissa went to her mother and hugged her. 'Hello,' she said. Her mother looked down at her fondly.

'You silly girl,' she replied.

A strange stillness hung over the house.

'Perhaps we're going to have a storm,' Lissa said.

'I don't think so, it's not that close,' Cass replied. They were standing at the window by Lissa's bed looking out over the countryside.

'Well, everything feels very strange. I suppose it's because Mr Hennessy is going.'

'I shall miss him. He was fun in the end,' Cass said. The sun had gone now and only the last red streaks were left. School was finished at last, and they had six glorious weeks to look forward to. Lissa stretched her arms over her head and yawned.

'I'm going to bed. See you in the morning.'

In the morning he was gone. The red car was no longer there and the cottage keys lay on the kitchen table.

Lissa looked at them and then at her mother as she ate her toast, wondering what her mother was thinking. There was an odd smile on her face, and she was humming quietly.

It was time to go and catch Sara and tack her up. Cass would be down soon. Outside it was a fine July morning.

The garden was taking shape nicely, the vegetables were growing, and all the roses were in bloom. Lissa did not know the names of all the flowers and shrubs in the garden but there were many of them. The air was filled with a sweet fresh perfume.

She walked round to the yard to fetch the tack and the grooming kit and heard a pony whickering. She gave a start of surprise, thinking that Sara must have broken out and wandered into the yard. But it was a different voice, a very familiar one, one which rose higher and higher until it became a squeal of excitement.

In the third box along, a head looked out, dark brown, with a mealy muzzle and a small white star between the eyes.

Lissa stared. It was not possible, she must be dreaming, but the pony called again and very slowly she walked towards him and held out a tentative hand, expecting the apparition to disappear. The soft velvet muzzle was real enough, and the insistent way he smelt her face and rubbed his nose against her neck was quite enough to convince her that her dream had come true.

'Merlin? Merlin?' she kept saying, although she could hardly speak. She unbolted the door and flung her arms round his neck. 'Merlin!' She untied the rope clipped to his headcollar and gently led him out into the yard, still not really believing that this could be true. Tears trickled out of the corners of her eyes and she wiped them away.

'Well, don't cry,' said Mrs Tallis, laughing. 'This is supposed to make you happy.' She had followed Lissa down to the yard, not wanting to miss the reunion. Cass was there as well.

'But how? I don't understand,' Lissa said.

'It's a long story. It began with that letter Cass had

from the girl at the stables. Cass and I were trying to think how we could manage it. I phoned Mrs Addison and she agreed to sell Merlin, but of course he was more than we could afford. We were really at our wits' end until that day Mr Hennessy asked if I would sell him two of those paintings. He gave me an excellent price for them, so I phoned Mrs Addison straight away and put a cheque in the post. She arranged the box from her end and Merlin arrived late last night. Cass had the loose-box ready and they unloaded him in the front while you were in bed. Mr Hennessy wanted us to wait until after he'd gone before we told you.'

'Merlin! I can't believe it.'

'So now I can have Sara all for my very own,' cried Cass. 'That's fair, isn't it?'

Lissa laughed, although she was still half-crying. 'I should say that's fair. Oh, I love him!'

'I'll go and catch Sara and we'll take them out together. It will be a good way of introducing them.' Cass scampered away in the direction of the field. Ginny went off to the cottage to practise her music, and Mrs Tallis had cooking to do.

Lissa fetched the grooming kit and with great delight began the process of brushing each familiar hair, using only a body brush on the velvet fur. The wild mane was in a tangle as usual and as she gently tried to sort it out Merlin kept turning his head to nuzzle her, seeming as amazed by this turn of events as Lissa was herself.

Sara, by now in her box, was neighing with excitement and reaching out her head to see who this new stable-mate could be.

'It is just impossible, she won't stand still,' Cass shouted. 'I'm going to tack up. I'll get yours as well.'

So then came the precious moment when Lissa put the bridle over Merlin's head, gently lifted the saddle on to his strong, willing back and fastened the girth. Leading him round the yard, Lissa knew there could never, ever, be a happier moment than this, no matter what was to come.